Advance Praise f

"*Tommy Gun Tango* is a masterful story of contrast, a perfect story for the economic times we're living through."
— Lesa Holstine, *Spinetingler's* Best Reviewer 2009

Praise for *PHILIPPINE FEVER*
from author Bruce Cook
USA BookNews Best Thriller Finalist 2006

"Fast paced and not for the faint of heart."
— *Bookbitch.com*

"If you enjoy fast-paced, gritty, thrillers set in exotic locations, this is a book that will have you turning pages as fast as you can."
— *Mystery Morgue Magazine*

"…authenticity in every page…"
— *Midwest Review of Book*s

Praise for *BLOOD HARVEST*
from author Brant Randall
USA BookNews Best Mystery Winner 2008

Reminiscent of *To Kill A Mockingbird*, … a chilling tale of the hatred, racism, and violence spread by the Ku Klux Klan, not in the South, but in New England in the early part of the last century.
— *Mystery Scene Review*

Tommy Gun Tango

A NOVEL OF HOLLYWOOD CRIME

Brant Randall / Bruce Cook

BRANT RANDALL

AND

BRUCE COOK

Capital Crime
PRESS

CAPITAL CRIME PRESS
FORT COLLINS, COLORADO

Disclaimer

This is a work of fiction. Names, characters, places, and incidents are the products of the author's imagination or are used fictitiously. Any resemblance to actual events, locales, or persons, living or dead, is entirely coincidental.

First edition published in the United States by Capital Crime Press. Printed in Canada.

Capital Crime Press is a registered trademark.

LCCN: 2009931775
ISBN-13: 978-0-9799960-3-0

www.capitalcrimepress.com

This is dedicated to the next
generation of storytellers in our family:
Ian, Sarah, and McKellan.

I want to acknowledge my debt to my fellow writers GF, SL, and RB. Their scrutiny and careful reading of the early drafts greatly improved this book. A special thanks to editor extraordinaire, Alex Cole.

A NOTE FROM ONE OF THE AUTHORS—

When my previous novel, *Blood Harvest*, was published many people asked what happened to the characters after that book ended. This book, *Tommy Gun Tango*, recounts the further events of three characters: Marshal Lawe, Jackie Sue, and Gladys.

Other readers wrote to ask why my characters sounded so "Southern" if they lived in Massachusetts. I am writing from the memory of my grandmother's speech patterns, a Scotch-Irish girl from the hills of Pennsylvania. Many urban dwellers hear no distinction between rural speech, hill speech, and Southern speech patterns, though they can easily distinguish between the Bronx, Brooklyn, and Queens. They hear it all as "country," just as most hill folk hear all urban speech as "city."

My earliest memories of my grandmother are of an upright, somewhat stern, proper woman in her forties, the woman who had made sure her three girls went to college. As Granny moved into her eighties and nineties she began to revert to the speech patterns of her youth, and I heard firsthand the echoes of Appalachia.

My grandmother was a true film fan. The family candy shop in Pennsylvania was next door to a movie theater that changed its bill daily. She attended several times a week. Later, when I studied cinema in college, I was able to hear her reminisce about audience reaction to the early films, from *Birth of a Nation*, to Chaplin and Keaton, and on into the talkies. About the time of Boris Karloff's *Frankenstein* (1932), my grandparents' business went bankrupt. They put their daughters in the family car, a Buick, and migrated to Los Angeles.

Like most Americans, they had never been across the

Rockies and were surprised by the ruggedness of the West. What they encountered in the city that became their new home that I have tried to depict in this book.

The easiest way to sum it up is this: From 1929 to 1933, the mayor of Los Angeles was a prominent West Coast leader of the KKK. He ran for office on the policy that Los Angeles would be the last bastion of native-born, white Protestantism. He was also a strict Prohibitionist and he abhorred the hedonistic motion picture industry, which boomed during these bleak economic times.

For this novel I have invented a gossip sheet, *The Hollywood Daily Tattler*, which closely resembles a number of sensationalist tabloids published about the movie industry in the 1920s. Although I created the paper, the stories I have placed in it are all factual, written in the style of the day. During my research I found contemporary newspaper accounts and court records to be invaluable in recreating the atmosphere of Hollywood during the Roaring Twenties.

This is the backdrop to a sensational true-life mystery. Did Jean Harlow's husband commit suicide or was he murdered? And if so, by whom?

After this tale is told I'll let my co-author have the last word.

Brant Randall
Castaic, California—about thirty miles north of Hollywood, as the crow (and rumor) flies, December 2008

P.S. The spiders are real. You'll know what I'm talking about when you get there.

1932

The Great Depression is in its third year.
Unemployment stands at 23.6%.
The Gross National Product has fallen 31% since
    Black Tuesday.
The top income tax rate rises to 63%, up from the
    previous 25%.
In July the Dow Jones trades at 41.22, a drop of 89%
    from its peak in September 1929.
Nearly one-third of all farms and homes are in
    foreclosure.
Three million homeless ride the rails and walk the
    roads looking for work.
A quarter of a million teenagers are among them.

MARSHAL LAWE

"Everything is funny
as long as it's happening
to somebody else."
—*Will Rogers*

one~
Bound for LA
12 July 1932

I'VE BEEN SHOT before. And I've taken my share of beatings. I was even left for dead once. But I'd never been beaten, shot, and buried alive in the same day.

I found I didn't much care for it.

I told the boss so and he told me to—

Wait. I'm getting ahead of myself. I need to tell you how I came to such a pass and why I ended up at Jean Harlow's place the day Paul Bern died.

You might want to get another beer. This could take a while.

~~~

I WAS INTO my third day of driving hard. I'd followed the Lincoln Highway through all the "burgs" of

Pennsylvania, crossed Ohio, then Indiana, hit Chicago, and was now dropping south on Route 66 toward Saint Lou. I only had eighty-seven dollars to get to Los Angeles and start my life over. That meant driving fourteen hours a day and sleeping by the side of the road, hoping I didn't throw a rod or blow a gasket or anything else that might put a fatal hole in my budget.

Some eighty miles out of Chicago, I pulled into the Sinclair gas station in Odell a bit after nine o'clock, rousting the kid who worked there from looking at a lurid issue of Clue magazine. He came out, scratching at a huge pimple in the middle of his forehead.

"Can you fill it up for me?" I said.

He stared at me like I was the one sporting a third eye.

"It's after hours. I was about to lock up."

And then he stood there with his mouth slightly open. Breathing, I guess.

"Well, seeing as how you ain't locked up yet, how about it?" Still polite, but feeling my etiquette beginning to wear thin.

"You're not from around here, no sir. What kind of accent is that?"

"Didn't your mother ever tell you to be polite to strangers?"

"There's no need to talk about my mother, no sir. I don't like that kind of talk from a hillbilly."

That was it. I took a quick step forward and grabbed the kid by the front of his shirt, pulled him close, messing up his bow tie.

"Folks who live in the Appalachians don't take to being called hillbillies. Seems disrespectful somehow." I realized I was going too far, so I eased up on his collar, allowed the kid to inhale again. "But I'm going to pretend I didn't hear what you said and let you fill my gas tank, check my tires, and clean my windows."

The kid like to wet hisself. Twice he filled the five-gallon glass atop the pump and let it drain into the tank of my Model A.

The stupid gas cap sat right in front of the windshield. I don't know what Henry Ford could have been thinking. Seemed like the pump jockey always spilled some and then you had to smell the fumes.

So I made sure Mister Pimple wiped everything spic and span before I paid my two dollar and eighteen cents. I drove off leaving him to tell a story on me to his boss.

I didn't care. I never planned to pass that way again.

I tried the radio, but I was too far from Chicago to get anything but static. I dialed around, searching for police calls, but got nothing.

two~
The Road to St. Louis

LOOKING BACK AT what happened next I now put it down to white line fever—that feeling that you're just floating along in your automobile and the dark fields are cruising by you. What with the heat of the day still lingering I had the windows down and the cicadas were roaring fit to drown out the sound of my tires. There was the smell of fresh-cut alfalfa with just a hint of cattle in the back of my nose.

Sort of lulls you to sleep.

And then some scarecrow with an orange mop for hair comes to life and lurches into the road with its thumb out and I clip his bindle as I jerk the wheel and the scarecrow twirls out of sight and my Fordor comes to rest in an irrigation ditch, wheels spinning free.

I sat there with the engine a-racing and my heart, too. Afeared I might have killed a man. I turned off the motor and climbed out, looking back into the darkness. Kind of hoping it was just a dream, pretty much sure it wasn't.

The jar flies had gone silent when the car crashed off

the road. I followed back along my tracks, trying to see by the red glow from my taillights. Couldn't see hardly nothing. Bit by bit the insects began their buzzing again, until I couldn't hear naught but my own footsteps.

So I leapt about three feet and lost several years from my lifespan when something gripped my shoulder.

"That was a close one, brother," said a voice from the darkness. "I thought I was after greeting the saints."

And that was Al Haine. He liked to dramatize the obvious. And that wasn't no mop. He stood about six-foot-three with a head full of hair the color of a baked yam.

After me recovering my wits and apologizing and us introducing ourselves, we set our shoulders to the bumper of my Ford and tried to get the rear wheels onto solid ground. Fifteen sweaty minutes later we give up on that and decided to roost for the night. Having nearly killed the fellow, I felt the least I could do was offer him a spot to rest his head inside my car, out of the night air.

He had a sandwich tied up in his bindle and solemnly offered to share it, for which I was grateful. I hadn't eaten dinner. Trying to save money, don't you know.

I ate in silence, but Al talked nonstop, and with an Irish brogue as dense as a thicket. I had to force my way through the underbrush to find his meaning, but I lost the trail half the time.

With all that blather it was hard to figure how he managed to talk, bite, and swallow simultaneous. When I finished my food, I held up my hand.

"I'd love to chew the fat with you some more, but I'm dead tired," I said. "That's how come I almost run you over. Let's call it a night and we can sort things out in the morning."

If I'd had any sense I would have seen that near miss as an omen of things to come.

~~~

WHEN I WOKE the sky had gone that peculiar gunmetal gray color that comes just before dawn. Al was missing, and I supposed it was his getting out of the auto that had awakened me. I hate to suspicion things, but I checked my wallet and the glove box to see if any of my goods was absent. He was gone, but nothing else was.

I resigned myself to waiting for a car to pass so I could hitch a ride to the nearest town and get some help. I settled my head against the seat back.

"Jaysus, Mary and Joseph!" said Al from somewhere outside.

I peered into the half light and saw him standing at the edge of a field, something in his hands. I felt under my seat, putting my hand on my service revolver.

"Ye didn't say you were the law," said Al, staring at the car door. "Ye only said your name was Lawe."

"I ain't a lawman now. Used to be, though. Look closer and you'll see the Potemkin County Marshall decals have been sanded off."

Al walked up and I saw that he was holding four ears of corn, still in their husks. He tucked them under his arm so he could run his hand over my old Ford's piebald paint job.

"I didn't know they sold used police cars. I was told they received a decent burial."

Thought he was funny.

"They called it my 'mustering out' pay when they cut my job." It also was payment to keep my head shut about a thing or two I knew regarding the county supervisors.

"Got the sack, did ye?" said Al.

That irritated me.

"No, I didn't get the sack. They closed the marshal's office when they moved the county seat. Said there wasn't enough local crime to keep a full-time officer."

He raised his eyebrows at that. "Ye must have lived in paradise, a town without crime."

"Wasn't much of a town when I left it. Peony Springs is mostly a farming community, and by then a third of the farms was foreclosed. Of course, that put an end to most of the businesses on Main Street."

"Foreclosed, were they?" He got a little steam in his voice. "Damn banks taking away the means of production from the working man."

"I don't know about that. The banks went under, too. Took my savings right with them."

"Ah, but where did your capital go to, brother? The farmland was still there, as fertile as ever. I dare say the farmers were still there, willing to work it. The bank building was still there, solid as a stone. The clerks were still there, happy to stamp your passbook."

He looked me in the eye, his face stormy.

"Suddenly the farmers had no farm, the bank was closed. You and the clerks, all of youse had no jobs. Mine is gone, too. But the capitalists still have their mansions, don't they? They still eat the fatted calf. Lenin had it about right." He began to wag an ear of corn, lecturing now. "Mark my word, the day is coming when their blood will run in the gutters, when the workers throw off their chains and—"

"Are we going to eat that corn, or you just going to wave it around?"

He stopped and settled himself, putting a sketchy smile in place.

"Of course, brother. The revolution must wait until we have fed. At the least."

I took an ear, skinned off the husk and stripped the silk with my fingers. I bit into those plump kernels, and I don't know when I ever have had something taste so good. Al did the same, though he stuffed the silk into the pocket of his plaid flannel shirt.

"You being a communist and all, I suppose you just liberated these ears from the field," I said.

Al took a big bite and chewed with gusto before he answered. "Property is theft, brother. I was helping save their souls from eternal damnation."

three~
Potholes in the Road

ONCE THE SUN was up—and after we had buried the shucks and cobs, thank goodness—a tractor come along the road. The wizened old codger driving a John Deere GP took a look at my car half in the ditch and half in the field. He pulled over and got down from his high seat without a word. He looked at the rear wheels grabbing air in the irrigation canal, then hooked a chain to the bumper and pulled the car back onto the road. Still without speaking he went to his knees and unhooked the chain.

His face had been sunbaked into a wrinkled roadmap, and I don't believe he had smiled since the last century. He looked at us and shook his head, as if to say, "These city slickers."

Al gave him the full blarney.

"Tis a wonderful day for the race, isn't it, sar?"

"The race?" The farmer's lips barely moved when he spoke, like he didn't want to waste energy on such a worthless pursuit. "What race would that be?"

"Why the human race, sar, on this fine and glorious day."

Farmer Brown—I call him that for convenience, since he never saw fit to give us his name—looked at the sky, then looked back at Al. He looked at the sky once more for good measure, then looked at Al to check his sanity.

"There's no rain coming. Nothing wonderful in that."

And of course he turned out to be the owner of the field where we'd spent the night. He felt it was a good joke to ask us a rental fee for our "campsite."

I give him a dime, which seemed to satisfy. For my part I figured that was cheap for a tractor tow and two breakfasts. Farmer Brown drove off without a backward glance. I expect he had a 'pointment to keep.

Anyhow we were back on the road. I had some hesitation about what I said next, but I knew last night had been a close call. I might not survive falling asleep at the wheel another time.

"Can you drive a car, Al?"

"Can birds fly?"

"All right then, I've got a proposal for you. I figure if we switch off driving, with the other sleeping, we can keep moving twenty-four hours a day and get there in just two days."

"Travel without a stop, you say?"

"We'll have to stop now and again for meals and fuel and to drain the snake, but still. No motel bills, fewer meals to pay for on the road."

"And where is it we're getting to, brother?"

"This is Route 66. I'm headed to Los Angeles."

"For me own part I'm headed away from Chicago.

Los Angeles sounds just right." Al hummed to himself, thinking about something humorous by his look. "Is it family you're having there?"

"Nope. And I've never been to the City of Angels before, but I heard the streets are paved with gold."

"I heard the same about America when I boarded the boat in Cork. I suppose it will be just as true in California."

"No call to be cynical."

"Cynical? The citizens themselves call it the Golden State, or so I've heard. Why should we be doubting them?"

Something about Mr. Haine didn't add up. In the daylight I could tell his clothes was none too clean, but he seemed to have bathed recently, and sprinkled on more eau de cologne than I thought was seemly. His shoes was broken in like they belonged to a working man, but I swear he was sportin' a manicure. What was he hiding?

Still, I was a man on a limited budget, and an extra driver would be a help.

~~~

IT TOOK ALMOST three days to reach California, so I'd been wrong in my calculations. There was a number of incidents along the way that ate up time. I'll get to those.

What with one thing and another I've been called garrulous on occasion. Once I met Al, I realized all such judgments are a matter of degree.

Al didn't sleep much and he seldom stopped talking. And if he wasn't talking, he was singing. He had an inexhaustible fund of Irish ballads. If I asked him to tone it down, he hummed to himself.

Not that he wasn't entertaining. He was. That man could spin a story that had you laughing one second and not two minutes later bring a tear to your eye. But I was never sure how much of them to believe.

We came to a mutual discovery: Driving for hours and hours in a closed space encourages men to share things they might not under other circumstances. I found myself telling him about my time as a marshal in Peony Springs. He expressed surprise to hear that the KKK was so strong in Massachusetts, powerful enough to lynch a man.

"I guess the klucks wasn't as strong as they thought they was," I told him. "Someone put paid to the local Klan leader right afterward."

Al mulled that over and then asked, "There were two murders in two days whilst you were on watch?" I could see he had his doubts about this. "And was it yourself brought the killers to justice?"

"Not exactly. Politics plays into murders and prosecutions more than you might think."

He looked thoughtful. "That's been my experience as well." I thought he might explain that, but he offered no further comment.

~~~

ANOTHER TIME WE talked about our respective names.

"Can you believe parents naming a child Ichabod Petrarch Lawe?" I said. "When I got old enough to realize the other kids was making fun of me, I asked my dad what it meant. 'The glory is gone,' he says. I must have looked kinda funny, so he added, 'Ichabod is Hebrew for the glory is gone.' And what about Petrarch, I asked. 'He was a great poet in his day, but no one remembers him now,' he said, like that explained things."

Al made a noise like he'd choked on a chicken bone, and I looked over to see what was wrong. He was stifling a laugh and couldn't look me in the eye. After a bit he spoke.

"I feel like I owe ye one. I may as well confess. Al is short for Aloysius. Ye try that one in the school yard, and ye'll find it's good for a bloody nose any time you like."

Al flipped a cigarette butt out the window and watched the sparks dance along behind us. "'Tis true what they say about parents. Ye can't live without them…and it ain't right to set 'em on fire. Though not all agree with that latter part."

I shot him a sideways look and he burst out laughing.

"You're too easy, Ichabod."

"You call me that again and you'll see how easy I am."

"Shall I be calling you Marshal, then?"

I agreed that would be best.

~~~

AL WAS TOO tall to sleep in the front seat, so he climbed into the rear and let his legs sprawl across the gray cloth back of the front bench. Later, when he shifted in his sleep, his pant leg rode up, and I saw that he had a sheath strapped to his calf, holding a wicked-looking serrated edge bowie knife.

My heart skipped a couple of beats and I broke a sweat, wondering just who I had in the car with me. Easy-like I reached over to relieve him of the weapon. No sooner had

I laid a featherweight on it, than his fist clamped around my wrist and he reared up from the back seat.

"Ye don't want to be touching that, Marshal," he said. "Private property is what that is. Just like that hog leg ye have stashed under the driver's seat." And then he give me a smile I don't care to see the like of again.

He put his head back down and said no more.

Neither did I.

The miles and hours drifted on by.

Once we got rolling along at a good clip he pulled out some newspaper he had stuffed inside his shirt. He caught me glancing at him in the rearview mirror, and said:

"I don't own a coat. This helps keep the warmth in."

He proceeded to tear a two-inch square, and then rolled a homemade cigarette from the corn silk in his pocket. When he lit up, the stink was something sinful. I angled the wind wing to blow the smoke away from me.

"Ye want me to roll ye one, brother? I've got some silk left."

I thought about the sweat-soaked paper that he'd just peeled off his ribcage and shook my head.

"You could have just asked for one of my Camels," I said. "I'm willing to share."

"I wouldn't want to put you out. Next time we stop I'll pick up some of my own smokes."

four~
Remembrance of Things Past

ANOTHER TIME I said, "I was heartsick that Gladys left, but hadn't the gumption to ask her to stay. My own prospects didn't look so hot. We wrote back and forth for a while, but I never know what to say in a letter, and finally things betwixt us just came to a halt. Prob'ly my fault."

"What made her leave?" said Al.

"This and that. We'd been sparking pretty steady after that KKK business and were starting to make plans. When the stock market crashed, her diner was hit hard. I saw things was bad, but I'd been through hard times before. I remember when the economy pretty much went to hell after the Great War, but it bounced back then, and I figured it would this time, too."

"So ye told her to look at the doughnut, not the hole?"

I nodded. "But neither Peony Springs, nor Potemkin County, nor the great state of Massachusetts—as I heard our blowhard senator say on the radio once—nor the US of A bounced back from this one. Wall Street took a dive, and that was imitated by some of the stock brokers."

"Far as I can see, stock prices ain't hit bottom yet," said Al, "though the brokers have."

"Crime dropped way off in Peony Springs. Wasn't nothing left to steal and most folks just stayed at home, looking grim. I didn't have much to do except for the occasional family disturbance."

"I tell ye, it's the international conspiracy of capitalists," said Al.

"I don't know about any conspiracy, but most folks lost all their money except what they had in the mattress when the bank failed. Then prices for produce and livestock dropped to twenty-five cents on the dollar from a year before. No one had any cash to spare for coffee and a doughnut, much less a dinner. First Gladys let her help go, then she was open only for lunch, and finally the bank foreclosed on her." I grimaced at the memory. "As marshal I had to deliver the eviction notice."

"Harsh."

"She went out to Los Angeles to stay with relatives. Heard there was work out there."

"So now you're following her?" said Al.

I thought about that for a bit. Was that what was really behind my moving to Los Angeles?

I shook my head. "No, though I certainly plan to look her up. It's just that there was nothing left for me in Peony Springs, either. I had to deliver foreclosures, auction notices, eviction papers to far too many of my friends and neighbors. And then oversee the sale of their goods. People I'd known all my life, left standing out in the street wearing everything they owned on their backs. It got so no one would look me in the face.

Crossed the street if they saw me walking their way."

"I'm telling ye, the revolution is coming sooner than ye think, brother."

"Folks moved away. The high mucky-mucks decided to relocate the county seat to a town that was still alive."

Reciting all this made my insides hurt.

"And just like that I was out of a job," I said. I didn't say so, but after being an officer of the law for twelve years, I was done with it. No more upholding of the law for me, no sir.

"But ye got the car, and at least they left the police radio in it," said Al. "We can eavesdrop on the fascists."

"I'd watch that kind of talk if I were you, Al. People have been lynched for less."

"I'll never see the end of a hangman's rope. I've got the luck of the Irish with me."

And he gave a sickly grin that made me think it might not be the luck of the Irish, but the curse. I wondered if a driving companion was such a bargain after all.

five~
Snake Eyes

"Wine is a peephole
on a man."
—*Alcaeus*

WHEN WE GOT to Foss in Oklahoma, I'd reached the end of my shift of driving. We fueled up at the Shell station, adding two quarts of oil, which hadn't been in my budget. I pulled over to the side of the road and climbed into the back seat. Al was looking kind of twitchy as he got out of the car.

"I saw a little store set back in those trees," said Al. "I'm going to see if I can buy some cigarettes."

As he walked into the twilight I watched him lean down and brush at his leg. I didn't know if he was pulling down his pant cuff or checking the knife he had there, but I couldn't keep my eyes open another second. I drifted off to the sound of crickets.

I don't know how long I slept. It was full dark when

Al woke me as he got behind the wheel and started the car. He looked into the back seat and saw I was awake. He tossed me two packs of Chesterfields, then squirreled the car onto the highway and floored it.

"That should make up for those corn silks," he said.

I sat upright and opened a pack, pulled out a coffin nail, and tamped down the loose ends. Al passed me a pack of matches advertising a place called the "Kit Kat Klub." I smelled the alcohol on him.

"Where'd you find something to drink?" I said. "This is the driest state I know of."

Al chuckled and pulled a small flask from his pants pocket. "Got it the same place I found the fags." He handed the liquor over the back of the seat.

When he did I saw that his lip was puffy and he had the makings of a shiner. I twisted off the top of the flask—it was nicely made, chrome plated, engraved with the initials RFB—and took a sip. It was corn liquor, but pretty raw and went down like a draught of lava, left me gasping.

I handed back the flask. I was worried about what had happened back in Foss.

"I thought you was just about broke, couldn't afford anything more than cigarettes."

Al uncapped the flask and took a deep swallow, then laughed at the burn.

"I had a streak of luck, me boyo."

"You call it luck that got you that fat lip and the black eye?"

He laughed. "Inconsequential, brother. 'Twas a minor dispute about whether I be allowed to leave the game without their having a chance to win back their stakes."

I noticed he looked into the side mirror as he said

this, so I took a glimpse out the back window. Couldn't see anyone following.

"What game would that be, Al?" I said.

"I went into that wee store just to buy a pack of ciga-reets. And what to my wondering eyes did appear but five men in their shirtsleeves with a pair of dice, kneeling on the floor, voices raised in a kind of prayer meeting. I made the decision on the spot that I could easily give up a pack of cigarettes if they would allow me to get into that crap game."

"So you made a bet? And won, I suppose."

"I ran my two bucks into seventeen, taking Robert's fags and flask to boot. It was the others laughing at him that turned the evening bellicose. Old Bob got in a lucky shot or two, but he was too far into his cups to be an effective pugilist."

"You're damn lucky no one had a gun with them. Lot of folks carry iron out here in the boondocks."

Al pounded the wheel in delight. "By Gawd, ye are a lawman! Ye called it perfect. It was the appearance of the pistol in Robert's hand that made me realize the friendly part of the game was over. I kicked the Colt out of his hand, breaking his finger I'm sure. The others tried to jump me, but they don't know the ways of the fighting Irish. I picked up a chair and laid about me with abandon, until the cheap article broke in me hands."

I noted that the more Al drunk, the more the Irish come out in his speech.

He chuckled at some memory of his battle and took another healthy swallow from the flask. Lowering it from his lips he shook it to gauge its contents, then offered it to me.

"There's but one gargle left, brother. It's for ye."

I took the flask and finished it off. "And how did you get away from five men?"

"Bob was howling in the corner, nursing his hand, and two more were unconscious after an encounter with a chair leg. I have to admit one of them laid hands upon me. It took a little pointed persuasion to make him let go."

A little pointed persuasion. Thought he was cute.

"If you stabbed someone, they'll call ahead to the next town and pull us over. I don't aim to spend time in an Oklahoma county jail."

About then we passed the sign that said we were within the township limits of Canute. I crawled into the front seat and switched on the radio. Once it warmed up I began searching for police calls at the top end of the dial. Nothing. I tried at the bottom end and got something, but it was too faint and there was too much static to make out what was being said.

"Take the next left you see," I said.

Al gave me a bloodshot glance.

"If we drop south a few miles on farm roads then turn west, we'll skirt around the next couple of towns."

I won't go into it any further except to say we got lost and spent three hours trying to find the way back to Route 66. That was one of our delays.

And I never was sure how much of his tale was true.

It might have been an armed robbery.

six~
Riparian Rites

THERE WERE TWO separate incidents in New Mexico that cost us time, and I have to admit one of them was my fault. It was a hot day and we passed a number of farm trucks overloaded with children and furnishings, families on the move to the West. I could see thunderclouds in the distance and hoped they would drop some rain on us, cool things down.

No such thing happened. It just got hotter and hotter.

We were close to Thoreau, right near the Continental Divide, when the radiator boiled over.

I got out, raised the hood, and tried to use my shirt-tail to undo the radiator cap. Steam and boiling water shot out, catching the edge of my hip and giving me a scald. My thick duck pants saved me from a serious burn.

We sat for an hour while the car cooled down, then drove slowly into town and pulled up to a white clapboard house that badly needed a coat of paint. A hose and bib was visible, so I went up on the porch and knocked at the screen door.

A petite woman with her gray hair pulled back tight and wearing a shapeless housedress came to the door. She looked at me with no welcome in her pale gray eyes.

"Don't need any odd jobs done," she said.

"I wasn't looking for work, ma'am. I just wanted to fill my radiator from your garden hose."

She looked at my Ford through the screen, paying attention to the sanded area on the door. She gave me a long look, as if to assess my worth. "I guess that's okay. Water'll cost you fifty cents."

I couldn't believe my ears. "Where I come from we give hospitality to strangers. I'm not asking for a handout. Water is freely shared."

"Then maybe you ought to go back where you come from and fill your radiator there. This is the desert and water is dear."

"You're charging me more for water than gasoline costs."

"You ever try drinking gasoline?"

"It's for my radiator," I said, my voice low so I wouldn't let the anger out. "It ain't worth fifty cents."

"If you're so smart, why don't you go another mile to the Whiting Brothers service station? Get your water there."

I was disgusted at her lack of human feeling. "I'll do just that." I turned my back on her.

"You'll find they charge a dollar for water." And with that she slammed the front door.

I walked back to the car and related my tale to Al. He shook his head.

"Ye lack the touch, brother. This is a job that requires Gaelic charm."

He trotted about fifty yards up the road to another

house. I watched him from the shade at the side of the car. I saw a kid in overalls open the door and Al began his blarney. A minute later the kid went inside and fetched his pa. The man took one look at Al and sharp words were exchanged, though I couldn't make them out. The father slammed the door in Al's face.

Being Irish, Al is always pretty pale, but I thought he looked extra white when he got back to the car.

"Said he'd have no truck with a red-haired mick," said Al. "What are the chances of meeting John Bull in New Mexico?"

"About the same as us paying a buck to fill our radiator," I said.

We limped a mile up the road, found the station, gassed up, paid to fill the radiator, and put in another quart of oil. I checked my wallet, tracking how much I'd have left to get started in the Golden State. Made me feel pretty low.

We stopped at a run-down diner with a battered counter and eight red Leatherette stools. Al was paying for the meals now, helping stretch my budget. We were able to get the daily special for a quarter each—meatloaf, spuds, green beans, and coffee.

Half an hour later we both felt better. I paid another thirty cents to buy a block of ice which we put in a nest of newspaper near the vent that brought fresh air into the Ford. That provided some cooling, and we were almost cheerful. Al wanted to see if he could find another crap game in a ramshackle roadhouse he spied at the edge of town, but I nixed that and we got back on the highway.

So of course we hadn't gone thirty miles before we had a blowout. The right front tire went flat in half a second and tugged us off the highway onto the shoulder. The spare was old and balding, but still sound, so I set about changing the tire.

I had time for a good think about whether I should invest in a new tire and reduce my capital, or take the risk of this tire also going bad, leaving us stranded in the Arizona wilds. I was sitting flat on my behind, my back to the desert, putting the wheel onto the drum when I heard Al off to my side.

I turned my head just in time to see him reach down, pull up his pant leg and slide that knife out smooth as butter. I thought about my pistol, but it was on the other side of the car and stashed under the seat. I hefted the tire iron, determined to make him pay if he came at me.

Quicker than I could follow, he threw his knife. I jerked back, so it whizzed by and thunked into the sand about six inches to my left. I moved to grab the knife and defend myself, but froze when I saw where it was stuck.

Pinned to the ground was the biggest spider I ever seen, the size of a cereal bowl, with hairy legs and a passel of eyes on its bulbous head. Them little pincers at the front was clicking frantic-like as it tried to wriggle away from the blade nailing it down.

"Put your right hand out, Marshal. Take that tire iron and sweep around to your left real quick as you stand up. I'll grab your hand and pull ye out of there."

"Have you lost your mind, Al? What will that accom—"

"This isn't the time for debate. Move now." And he stretched out his hand toward me.

I did what he said and he about jerked my arm from its socket. Once I was on my feet and facing his direction I saw them.

Hundreds and hundreds of these spiders was coming

out from under the desert brush, heading for us. Al stretched as far as he could, left hand holding onto the bumper, and retrieved his bowie. I began to flail about with the tire iron, and the sound it made when I squished the critters made that meatloaf dinner want to come up.

The road was filling up quick and pretty soon they was all around us, a writhing carpet of black. They run faster than I'd ever seen spiders move, and occasionally one jumped maybe a foot into the air. One even leapt onto the running board of the car.

"We better get inside and close the car doors," I said.

Al and I got into the Ford, me in the front, him in the back, slamming the doors on a couple of them. Al stuck his head out the window to see what was happening, but then he saw one had moved up the running board and was climbing the slope of the fenders. In a few seconds it'd be at the same level as the windows. We rolled them up and pulled the wind wings shut.

"I cut one in half with my knife and both sides walked away," said Al.

I give him a look. "No, they didn't. It ain't anatomically possible for one half of a spider to walk without the other half."

Al laughed. "Ye caught me, brother." He winked. "But the next person who hears that story will be a believer, or I'm not the man I think I am."

The car heated up in the late afternoon sun, but we dassen't open a window. I recognized the creatures as tarantulas, but I'd never seen them that size or in that number. We talked about why they might be migrating across a highway.

"Ye don't suppose they've found a shortcut to California, do ye?"

At last the spiders all passed. I got the wheel mounted and we drove the last leg to Beulah Land.

seven~
West Coast Skyscrapers

ONE OF THE problems of driving up to Los Angeles—or LA, as the natives call it—was that I wasn't sure when I was all the way there. Starting about Cucamonga, the town names came together ever closer. Upland, Claremont, La Verne, Glendora—a cascade of places that pert nigh blended one into another, all with a range of mountains running alongside.

And these were real mountains, not like the Berkshires back home in Massachusetts. Why those are just puny hills compared to the San Gabriels. These stand close to ten thousand feet.

Al was agog as he looked up at them. Told me the tallest mountain in all of Ireland was just a tad over three thousand.

Orange groves, everywhere we looked, full of luscious-looking globes. And the wild mustard covering the hills with their yellow blooms.

I thought we had arrived when I caught sight of a fine-looking city hall, built in the Italian style, but it turned out to be Pasadena. There was still a bit to go. Went through a pass in some hills and there stood a skyscraper, Los Angeles City Hall, all thirty-two stories.

Al and I had both been to New York City a time or two, so we'd seen tall buildings before. But they was all crowded together in Manhattan. Didn't leave a fellow room to breathe.

Now LA, that was something different. Room to move around. Mountains, the Pacific Ocean, fruit growing everywhere in the valleys.

Plus the sunshine. I began to believe it truly was the Golden State.

~~~

IT WAS ABOUT lunch time, so Al and I stopped into a basement dive called Phillipés near Chinatown. Trestle tables, sawdust on the floor, two-cent coffee, and sammiches for two dimes. I had a French dip with lamb and Swiss cheese that made me think I'd died and gone to heaven. Al had hisself a ten-cent bowl of stew that seemed to satisfy, if I can judge by the way he smacked his lips.

I seldom seen such a lively place. There was a back room with a group of carney folk carrying on pretty loud. And out front a bunch of athletes wearing letter sweaters from the University of Southern California was staging some species of eating contest, seeing who could down the most pickled pigs' feet. I also saw a lot of traffic going up the staircase. I figured it was the waterloo and decided to pay it a visit.

Once I got upstairs I found some enterprising soul was selling bootleg out of a closet. Had him a steady stream of customers. LA was turning out to be interesting. I found the john and wrung it out, then went back downstairs.

When I rejoined Al I saw that plenty of boys in blue had come in for lunch. Hard to believe they didn't know what was happening upstairs, but nothing come of it. Seemed to make Al nervous, but I figured the place was safe from organized crime if the cops was there. We finished our coffee and left.

When we got outside a policeman was standing by my Ford, writing in a bitty notebook. Al took one gander and walked on by like he wasn't with me. I pulled up next to the policeman.

"Some problem, Officer?" I said.

"This car belong to you?"

I nodded.

"Why you driving a police car with Massachusetts plates?"

"I used to be a marshal in Potemkin County, Massachusetts. They cut my job and the car is mine now. They had me sand off the official insignia."

"And why are you in Los Angeles?"

"I heard it was the land of opportunity."

"You trying to be smart?"

"Not a-tall. I'm looking for work."

"Let me see your license."

I was starting to get a little hot under the collar, but I pulled out my billfold and showed it to him. He copied down my particulars and then had me fetch the car registration.

"Where will I be able to find you?" said the officer.

"I haven't got a place to live yet. I just arrived an hour ago."

"That so?" He thought for moment and then wrote an address in his notebook, tore off the sheet and handed it to me. "This place is clean, run by decent folk. You can get a room at the Kipling by the week pretty cheap. And they have a phone. I'm going to want to hear from you, that you have a job and place to live. Our city doesn't tolerate vagrants."

This seemed like a mild shakedown to me, but if the hotel was cheap and clean, I didn't see the harm. If it wasn't, I'd slide away.

"You call the Rampart Precinct and ask for Halliday." He took back the slip and jotted a phone number.

"Sure."

"Cause I'm going to check this registration with Potemkin County, see if it's valid."

He flipped his notebook shut and walked downstairs into the sammich shop.

I got into the car. Once the local flatfoot was gone, Al come on back and climbed in from the opposite side.

Al had a disgusted look on his face. "Cops." And a moment later, "Present company excepted."

eight~
Going Hollywood

WE DROVE WEST on Third Street, and when we crossed Normandie Al give a hoot and pointed out the window. I looked and saw a big white set of letters on the mountainside that said "Hollywoodland."

"I'll be. Them letters must be fifty foot tall."

"These Californians think big," said Al.

We found the Kipling Hotel just past Normandie. Looked all right, nothing fancy. Had a little awning over the sidewalk like they was expecting rain. Maybe in Los Angeles it's to keep the sun off instead of the wet. I pulled over to the curb. We got out and I retrieved my suitcase from the trunk.

"Do ye think this place is named after the British author?" said Al.

"I s'pose we can go inside and ask them. What's it to you?"

"I never cared for his stories of the Empire. They smack too much of the condescension I suffered in Ireland."

"I didn't know you were such a reader. I took

you more for a hummer, from my experience."

Al shot me a look that said I should keep such opinions to myself. I followed him into the lobby, where we waited a goodish time for the clerk, a young man in a gabardine coat and cheap—but colorful—tie, to finish a lengthy conversation with his bookie. Seems the dogs was running that day out at the Culver City Kennel Club. Al's ears pricked up as he listened in.

While we cooled our heels I said to Al, "We can't go seeking gainful employment if we look like hobos. This gives us a chance to get our clothes washed and pressed." I jerked a thumb at the clerk. "Besides, the hotel has a telephone. Maybe we can tip him, use it to get calls about work."

So the two of us split the cost of a week's rent—three dollars fifty cents each—and arranged to have an extra fold-out cot brought in. Had our hair cut and shoes shined—not that it did much good, beat up as they were. I checked my wallet and thought I better find work tomorrow or the next day at the latest.

After the elevator boy took us to our rooms, we asked him to go down the street to the Woolworths and get some lunch to carry out. He was a colored fella, about fifty, by the name of Clarence. He had a gimpy leg, and he'd cut his hair so short it looked like black prickles under his cap. He seemed friendly enough.

"This ain't going to be a problem for you, buying food at the counter there?" I said.

His eyes got a little distant. "What do you mean, sir?"

"I just moved here and I don't know the lay of the land yet. Some places a colored boy tries to buy somewhat to eat, and they don't want to serve him."

"This ain't the South," he said. "That's why I moved here." He looked peevish. "And that's a fact."

"Say, I didn't mean to offend. I was just trying to avoid trouble. For either of us."

He softened up a bit. "Of course, sir. I'll be back directly with your meals."

The chambermaid took our laundry. We sat in our underwear and read through the Herald and Express newspaper looking for jobs while our duds was made presentable. Poor Al had only his plaid flannel and one more shirt, his work pants and two pair of socks. Course I wasn't that much better off, but at least I had a coat and hat.

I discovered a couple of likely prospects in the classified ads. Al seemed more interested in the gossip columns and celebrity news. He looked up from the paper with a smile.

"When I was a lad in Antrim I was a big fan of the fillums. I loved it when a new Charlie Chaplin played at the cinema," he said. "They'd have that cardboard statue of him outside, saying 'I am here today.' Used to go with me mam, her carrying a babby on her hip. Now here I am in the city where all these moving pictures were made. 'Tis a great thing, it is."

I hoped he wasn't going to wax nostalgic and tell me more stories of his boyhood in Eire, so I changed the subject quick.

"I see they're looking for a man can ride a mule and handle a gun someplace up on Fleming Street. I growed up doing both, so I believe I'm going to apply for that one. Means I'll be headed north toward Hollywood. You find anyplace where I might drop you?"

"I think I'll make my way into Culver City and see

if the canines are racing tomorrow. I heard the streetcar only costs a nickel."

I shook my head. I could read him like a book. Thought he'd gamble the few bucks he had left and make a score.

~~~

I FOUND THE studio on Fleming Street in east Hollywood, a nondescript area of warehouses mixed with apartments and residences. I parked and made my way into the office. When it was discovered I knew which end of a horse did the eating, Monogram Pictures hired me on the spot. They drove me out to a spot in the Santa Clarita Valley about thirty miles north of LA, and I was put to work on a western starring Bill Cody.

He turned out to be a decent fellow from St. Paul, wore a huge Stetson, the ten-gallon variety. He sat near me during lunch that first day, which was served chuck wagon style under some live oak trees. He seemed to prefer the company of the animal handlers to the other actors.

"I know you must have heard this before, but Buffalo Bill died when I was a teenager," I said. "Nineteen-sixteen or -seventeen, I seem to recall."

He sort of smiled and finished chewing a fine piece of steak they'd served us. "My family name is Cody. When my parents saw his Wild West show they thought it would be just wonderful to name me Bill."

"Must have turned some heads when you come to town."

"First movie company that hired me thought I was the real Buffalo Bill. When I told them I wasn't even related, they billed me as the 'reel' Bill Cody, supposedly to clarify things. My belief is they wanted to add to the public's confusion."

We got on fine, and he was interested to hear about some of my cases as a marshal back East. I even told him about the KKK in Massachusetts.

"It's much the same in Minnesota," he said. "I got a brother-in-law is a Kluxer."

"Minnesota's got 'em, too?" I shifted on my seat, a little unsettled by this news. "Like fleas on a dog."

He give me a funny look. "I'm guessing you haven't heard about our mayor here in Los Angeles, then."

I nodded my head no.

"Porter's a strict Prohibitionist. He also used to be head of the KKK here in Southern California. He had an interesting plank in his campaign platform. Says Los Angeles is the last bastion of native-born white Protestantism."

"Native-born? Sort of passing over the Indians and all the Mexicans who live here? I was kind of hoping I was shet of that malarkey."

"Welcome to LA."

I chewed things over a bit and said, "The elevator boy at my hotel allowed as how things was way better here than in the South."

"Well, maybe they are," said Bill.

We shook our heads over that, and then the assistant director hollered that lunch was over.

Five days passed before I got back to the Kipling. I left a message for Al with the desk clerk on the third day, but wasn't sure if he got it or not. I also took time to send a postcard to Gladys at the last address I had for her, giving her the hotel telephone number.

I was hoping she'd call. Maybe we could get things back on track.

~~~

SAY, SINCE THE Great War I never worked so hard or got so dirty as I did making movies. If I wasn't feeding horses and mules, I was saddling them. Or wiping them down and putting them away. Or mucking out the stalls and watering the stock. It went on sixteen hours straight, and by then I was so tuckered out I just slept in a stall in the barn, since I had to be back on "set," as they called it, by five o'clock in the ayem.

The third day they made me a background actor. Seems they needed an "extra" cowboy to drive some cows through the background while the stars said their lines in front of the camera. What it really meant was they got me to do two jobs for the price of one, because after I was on camera all day, I still had to wrangle the stock and clean the stable.

The fourth day was more of the same, but on Saturday I was asked if I would like to partake in a bar fight for the film, get my picture took.

"What's the extra pay going to be? I don't need any more chores for no pay."

"Five dollars on top of the five dollars you're already making for the day. You report to wardrobe now. After you're in costume see the stunt coordinator and learn how the fight works, OK?"

Ten dollars? Sure, I wanted to be a "stunt" fighter.

I got dressed, and then some young gal with greasy hair and powerful BO put makeup on me, which made me feel pretty peculiar. I looked at myself in the mirror and hoped no one would recognize me back home if this western made it to the Odeon, our local theater.

I spent about half an hour rehearsing a fight sequence with the stunt coordinator, a small Prussian with a badly sunburned nose. He was a no-nonsense veteran from the other side of the Great War who had taught hand-to-hand combat, knew his business. I have to say it seemed easy enough to me.

"You are being just some thirsty cowpoke going into a saloon for to drink," he said. "Ah! But it seems there is a brawl already in progress. You up on the bar jump and this balsa wood chair swing at the fellow in the maroon vest."

The cameras was put into place and the lights was finally set and they hollered "Action!" and a few seconds later I was given the high sign to go through the swinging doors. Inside there was about thirty guys mixing it up pretty good, so I hoisted myself onto the bar, look around for the feller in the maroon vest and hit him with the breakaway prop chair just like I was told.

I'm guessing they hadn't told the other fellow. When I whanged him over the head, he turned on me like a cornered polecat, swarmed up on the bar, and began to swing at me. I cried out, "It's all part of the movie!" but his dander was up. Besides, the director was loving it.

Eventually they called "Cut!" and we had lunch under the trees again.

I sat with three other extras from the fight scene. I noted that they all sported bruises and had some trouble chewing their food. About then the assistant director come over with some paperwork to sign. He was the kind of guy who thought he brought sunshine into the world by his very presence. He seen how glum we was, so he decided to improve our dispositions.

"You fellows know what you get when you cross a frog with a dog?"

My three compadres looked at him like they'd had a glimpse of purgatory. He turned his attention to me.

"Well, do you?" he said.

"I bet you're gonna tell me, ain't ya?"

"Sure. I wouldn't want to leave you hanging. It's a dog that can lick itself from across the room." He beamed at us, flashing a gold tooth.

Not a chuckle. The four of us extras got back to eating.

He went away all huffy, saying under his breath, "There's no helping such people."

Next scene after lunch they had a bad guy take a shot at me with some "blanks," as they call them. I can tell you, the wad of paper that comes out of the gun barrel is red hot and it stings like the devil. "Blank" don't begin to describe it.

Like I said before, I've taken beatings a time or two. And I'd been wounded in the war. In the final scene of the day's photography I was supposed to be unconscious and the villains was digging a shallow grave for their victim. I was going to be buried alive.

I wasn't too happy about this, since I got the closet-phobia, you know, fear of small places.

The guy doing the spade work thought he was a comedian. Once I got that first shovel of dirt in the face—the jerk said it was an accident—I was done with being a stunt man. I boiled up out of that hole and went after Mister Shovel. The other stuntmen broke it up and I left the set in a hurry.

I went and told the boss a few things.

"I don't care to be beaten, shot, and buried alive in

the same day." I was beginning to think that shoveling horse hockey was comparing pretty good to this stunt business.

The boss was a little string bean of a man with a sty in one eye and permanent dyspepsia.

"Pick up your check and don't come back. I don't need extras or stunt men who can't follow instructions."

nine~
All's Well That Ends
22 July 1932

ABOUT MIDNIGHT I got back to the hotel, sent my clothes out for laundering, and soaked myself in a hot bath until the aches began to ease some.

It was one in the morning when I heard the door open. I still had the warshrag over my face when Al began to sing from the other room:

> "Alas and well may Erin weep, that Connaught lies in slumber deep.
> But hark, a voice like thunder spake, the west's awake, the west's awake!
> Sing, Oh hurrah! Let England quake, we'll watch till death for Erin's sake."

"Stop that bellowing, Al. There's folks who want to sleep," I called out.

The bathroom door swung open. Al leaned against the jamb and blinked at me. I seen that he had a snootful and was feeling little, if any, pain.

I jerked the drain plug and grabbed a towel. Al pulled his chrome flask from the hip pocket of a new pair of pants and upended it. He also had on a new Arrow shirt and some classy brogues, freshly shined. From the smell of it, that was a good Cuban cigar he was smoking.

"You're looking stylish," I said.

"The fates have been kind. I backed a lean courser by the name of Finn MacCool at the Kennel Club and came away a new man." He paused to wag his finger at me. "Ye would have done well to follow in me footsteps, young Marshal. Me speculations at the track allowed me to renew the wardrobe and treat fellow adventurers to a round of libations."

"I prefer to be gainfully employed. My luck ain't that great. Wasn't for bad luck I wouldn't have any a-tall."

Al stretched out on his bed without bothering to undress any more than kicking off his shoes. I slid between my sheets, clean for the first time in three days. Wasn't but ten seconds before I was out.

~~~

IT WAS SOME two hours later when there came a sharp rapping at the door. I woke from a dead sleep not sure what was happening. The sound came again and I sat bolt upright. A little slash of light from the streetlamp came through the window and lay across Al's face. With the third set of raps I saw him wince in his sleep and a look of fear flashed across his face, but he didn't wake.

"Mr. Lawe," I heard, the sound muffled by the door. "Mr. Lawe."

I pulled on some clean dungarees, went to the door

and pulled it open a crack. The desk clerk stood there, his clothes a little disheveled as if he too had been awakened.

"What?"

"There's a woman on the phone. Claims it's an emergency."

"A woman?"

"Says her name's Gladys."

"I'll be down in a minute."

I pulled on a fresh undershirt, slipped on my shoes and headed downstairs. When I picked up the telephone receiver, the line had gone dead, but the clerk had thought to write down the number and I called back.

A woman's voice came on the line, nasal and snake-mean. I put it down to the time of night. I felt kind of cranky myself.

"Los Angeles Police Department, South Central Division."

"I'm not sure I got the right number."

"Why don't you call back when you are sure," said Miss Snake.

"No, hang on. I'm looking for a Miss Gladys Alwin. Does she work there?" I said.

"No one by that name on our roster." There a sound of shuffling paper. "But they did bring in a pinky by that name."

"A pinky? What are you talking about?"

There was a pause and then, "I'll have her brought to the phone by an officer."

I heard the phone receiver clunk down on a countertop and there was longish wait with voices in the background, but nothing I could make out. At last the receiver was picked up again.

"Yes?" said Gladys. Her voice was tired, but it still gave me a little thrill to hear it. "Who is it?"

"Gladys, it's me. You put in a call for me a while ago. What's happened?"

She tried to speak but started crying instead. I heard Snake Voice in the background say, "You only get three minutes. I'd make them count, if I were you."

There was some snuffling and I recognized the sound of Gladys blowing her nose. "Petey."

She's the only one calls me that. No one else is allowed to do so.

"Petey. They've locked me up and there was no one else I could call."

"What are you talking about? You're the last person ever needed locking up. What's the charge?"

"Charge? They haven't told me. They asked a lot of questions and now they won't let me go home."

"If they haven't charged you, they can't keep you there."

"They said they were waiting for the detective to come in and interrogate me." She broke off and began crying again. "I'm afraid of him, Petey, I'm afraid of what he's going to do."

"Put that woman back on the line. I'll straighten this out."

Well, I tried, but I couldn't. Something big was happening, and they weren't about to tell me what it was. I realized I had to drive on down to South Central and find out why they were holding the woman I cared about. No, it was more than just cared about. The woman I loved.

When I said it to myself, I realized it was true.

I was dressed and on my way in ten minutes.

MISS ILONA'S HOLLYWOOD SCRAPBOOK
PART I: *FATTY ARBUCKLE*

HOLLYWOOD'S DAILY TATTLER

FATTY ARBUCKLE UP FOR MURDER!
--Sept 17, 1921

Roscoe "Fatty" Arbuckle, 34, was arraigned today for the murder and rape of actress Virginia Rappe, 30. San Francisco District Attorney Matthew Brady will handle the prosecution personally. A little bird tells us the DA plans to run for governor and thinks the publicity won't hurt a bit.

Adolph Zukor, head of Paramount Pictures, said that it "was a very sad occurrence, but I am sure Roscoe was innocent of any wrongdoing." *The Daily Tattler* reported only last month that Zukor had signed Fatty to a one million dollar per year contract for three years.

Arbuckle recently completed three pictures simultaneously and on September 5 went to San Francisco with friends to celebrate. During a party at the Saint Francis Hotel Miss Rappe was injured. She died four days later at Wakefield Sanatorium, a maternity hospital known to administer abortions...

SENSATIONAL DETAILS OF FATTY MURDER TRIAL!

--November 25, 1921

In his opening statement DA Brady theorized that Roscoe Arbuckle's immense weight crushed Virginia Rappe while he was raping her, rupturing her bladder. The subsequent infection killed the girl.

First prosecution witness Betty Campbell, who says her occupation is "model," testified that she saw Fatty with a smile on his face just hours after the alleged rape. Under oath Nurse Grace Hultson said she believed that Arbuckle's weight and the violence of the rape caused the extensive bruising to Miss Rappe's body.

Under cross-examination defense attorney Gavin McNabb got Hultson to admit that the bladder may have ruptured because of cancer and that the bruises may have been caused by the heavy jewelry Rappe was wearing that evening...

FATTY MISTRIAL: JURY DEADLOCKED!
--December 4, 1921

With the jury voting 10-2 to acquit Arbuckle, the judge has declared a mistrial. DA Brady immediately demanded a new trial, which is set for January 1922...

NEW FATTY TRIAL: PERJURY?
--January 24, 1922

Sensational articles run by Hearst's papers charge that Arbuckle raped the young woman with a chunk of ice. Others speculate that the object used to violate her was a champagne bottle.

Meanwhile witnesses from the first trial are changing their testimony. Zev Pevron says that DA Brady forced her to lie. Betty Campbell, "model," says that Brady threatened to charge her with perjury if she refused to testify against Arbuckle. Criminologist Dr Heinrich says the fingerprint evidence he analyzed putting Arbuckle and Rappe in the same room may have been faked.

The case for the prosecution seems so flimsy that the defense has decided not to bother with testimony from Arbuckle...

SECOND FATTY MISTRIAL!
--February 4, 1922

Much of the jury seems to have interpreted Arbuckle's refusal to testify as a sign of guilt. They returned a split vote of 10-2 guilty, deadlocked again. A mistrial was declared.

DA Brady insists there will be a third trial...

ANOTHER FATTY SPECTACLE!
--April 24, 1922

With seven months of constant sensational coverage by the Hearst syndicate and innumerable editorials condemning the vices of Hollywood, Fatty Arbuckle's third trial got under way. There was an immediate sensation when it was found that key prosecution witness Zey Pevron has fled the country.

This time Fatty testified in his own behalf and spoke convincingly to the jury. Medical experts opined that the fatal bladder rupture may have been the result of an abortion Miss Rappe had a short time before the party.

The jury took but six minutes to acquit Fatty of murder and rape. They took another five minutes to write a letter of apology to Mr. Arbuckle:

"Acquittal is not enough for Roscoe Arbuckle. We feel that a great injustice has been done him ... there was not the slightest proof adduced to connect him in any way with the commission of a crime. He was manly throughout the case and told a straightforward story which we all believe. We wish him success and hope that the American

people will take the judgment of fourteen men and women that Roscoe Arbuckle is entirely innocent and free from all blame."

Because of his testimony that alcohol was present at the party, Arbuckle pled guilty to violating the Volstead Act and paid a fine of $500. He is said to owe $700,000 in legal fees. His films are now banned throughout the world and his contract with Paramount has been repudiated. Mr. Hayes of the Motion Pictures Producers and Distributors Censor board has banned Fatty from ever working in US movies again.

The Daily Tattler asks: Isn't this bad for the movie business? When will producers learn to control their employees?

GLADYS ALWYN

"O would some Power the giftie gie us
to see ourselves as others see us."
—*Robert Burns*

one~
Hummingbird Café
June 1932

I WAS COOKING over to the Hummingbird Café on east
Twelfth Street, a sweet little jazz club and restaurant. It
was a Negro joint—the customers, the band, the waiters,
the owner, the cooks. Being such a light-skinned woman, I
took a lot of guff from the staff, so I tried to keep my head
down. I was just as happy to be working in the kitchen,
listening to the music coming over the slide where I put
the dishes up for the waiters.

One night I heard some boogie so hot I poked my head
through the window. I saw the owner, Tessie Patterson,
snapping her fingers along with the music. Tessie was
still a fine-looking woman, but somebody needed to tell
her that dress she almost had on was cut for someone
smaller. Wasn't going to be me, though.

"Who's that playing?" I said.

"You don' recognize that stride piano? That Jelly Roll Morton."

The men at the tables began hooting, as they watched some of the gals doing the Lindy Hop.

"If he bangs that piano any harder, it's going to come apart at the seams," I said.

"Yes, yes. That man lay down a mean bass line," said Tessie.

The crowd began stomping the wooden floor in time to the music. Lucky for us the café had no neighbors near enough to call the police.

I went back to the range, flipping steaks to the beat.

Now the Hummingbird sold its share of hooch, or it couldn't have stayed in business. I'm not a big drinker so I never sampled their wares, but I kept hearing they served pretty good stuff.

I suppose it was the combination of jazz and liquor that brought in the criminal crowd. The men dressed in the most beautiful camel hair coats, over perfectly cut suits. They arrived in gleaming Cadillacs and Lincolns, always accompanied by gorgeous women in expensive gowns, nails lacquered blood red, and their hair marcelled and glossy.

Like most cities, I suppose, the coloreds and the whites in Los Angeles each had their own crime bosses. Uncle Anton ran the Negro criminal element in LA. He controlled the numbers racket for South Central, most of the marijuana, and his men ran the prostitutes that served the colored areas of the city, but also provided call girls to the Hollywood set.

Uncle Anton stood six-foot-seven and must have weighed over three hundred pounds. He wore suits made of cashmere wool that were soft as butter, usually navy blue in winter and cream colored in summer. Unlike many of his lieutenants who wore flashy diamond rings on several fingers, Uncle wore no jewelry on his person. His trademark was a stick pin with a three carat pink diamond set in a lover's knot of pure gold. It was said to have been stolen from an English duke while he was travelling in South America, and to have cost three men and a woman their lives before it came into Uncle's possession.

I don't know about that, but I do know it was the most beautiful stone I have ever seen. And I saw it up close. It happened like this:

One of the men running call girls for Uncle Anton was "Skin'n Bones" Jones. Unfortunately for me, Bones caught a glimpse of me through the kitchen door. There is always a certain demand for colored hookers who can pass as white. It let some rich white man pretend he is walking on the wild side by bedding a Negro, yet didn't scare him too much either, because the girl didn't look all that different from a brunette of his own race.

One night about eleven-thirty, I was cleaning the grill. We had shut down the kitchen and the bar was serving drinks only until closing. I was hard at work, scrubbing the expanse of steel with a pumice brick, when Jones came up behind me and put his arm around my waist.

"What's a fine girl like you doing in the kitchen?" he said, his breath moist in my ear.

I spun around and pushed him away. "What the hell you think you're up to? Keep your hands to yourself."

One of the problems with Jones was that he's all flash and no brains. He thought I just needed persuasion.

"What's your name, pinky? I can get you out of this

kitchen and into a beautiful apartment, dress you up, and you be makin' a hunnerd dollahs a week. You be drinkin' fine wine and eating caviar in no time."

"Get your bony ass out of this kitchen right now, or you're going to rue this day."

I called out to the pearl diver, a tall drink of water who was a little slow mentally, but who liked me because I didn't make fun of him.

"Rufus! You going to let this man put his hands on me?"

Jones looked at Rufus and laughed out loud, seeing him standing there like he was a statue. I saw that Rufus was too afraid of Jones to help me out.

That was about the time Jones leaned in and grabbed my buttocks.

"You got some money-makers here, girl."

I reached behind me and got a cast-iron frying pan by the handle. I was too close to get a full swing but when I connected with his head you could hear the *clang* out front.

Jones staggered back and began to holler that he'd been kilt. He pulled a knife and come at me, though he was a little wobbly on his feet.

This was all too much for Rufus. He bellowed like a heifer that had snagged its udder on the bobwire, and then he ran out the rear exit. Tessie came through the swinging door, followed by several men, but by now I was fired up, and I began swinging that fry pan at Jones again and again. I knocked the knife out of his hand and hit him in the short ribs twice and was fixing to rearrange his face when suddenly I was grabbed and smothered.

Uncle Anton had me crushed against his chest, squeezing the breath out of me. When I tried to take a breath I was overpowered by the scent of his pomade. All I could see clearly was that pink diamond stickpin, not six inches from my nose. I could hear his deep rumbling voice coming through the wall of his chest.

"What's this fuss all about?"

I would have answered if I had any breath left in me. I heard Jones go quiet and as I squirmed around so I could see, I found that Uncle had his giant hand locked around Jones' throat. Jones' eyes was bugging and his mouth was working like a goldfish.

I gave a muffled groan and Uncle eased up on me a little.

"He made a nasty proposition," I said. "Then he grabbed my behind, like I was one of his whores. And I ain't his whore or anyone else's."

Anton turned loose of me altogether, let go of Jones' throat and clamped a ham-sized hand on each of Jones' shoulders.

"Jones, I tole you before. You don't be trying to force wimmins into the life. They's enough volunteers."

Jones took a deep shuddering breath, seemed about to speak, then caught a glare from Uncle. He shut his mouth tight, though he looked daggers at me.

Uncle saw that and began shaking Jones like he was some rag doll. Jones' head snapped back and forth and I heard his neck popping.

"Dammit, Jones. You be givin' this little girl any trouble I gonna kick yo' skeleton ass into next week. Now get back out front."

Jones dragged himself out of the kitchen, looking as sorry as a beat dog. Anton looked at me, took the frying pan out of my hand—I had forgotten I still had hold of it—and went to our big icebox. He opened the door, looked around to see what was in there, and took out a platter of fried chicken, about enough for six people.

As he walked out he looked over his shoulder at me and said, "He won't give you no mo' problems."

But something told me this was just the beginning of my troubles.

two~
Watts
January 1931

COOKING FOR A LIVING never done anyone any harm. It's honest work and no matter how bad times are, you always can find some restaurant or other needs a cook. It had only taken me a week to find a situation for myself in Los Angeles when I first got there in '31.

Still, that was one of the longest weeks of my life, moving in with my Great-Aunt Naomi, having her tell me what I ought to do; what was wrong with what I've already done; where I was going to end up if I didn't correct my ways; why I was a shame to my family and my race; why I needed to find a solid Negro husband, birth me some darker children, and help erase my mother's sins.

Sure it was room and board, but everything has a price.

"Girl, you need to get yourself a job. I can't feed no extra moufs."

Although Aunt Naomi talked rough, I knew she

wouldn't throw me out. I answered back easy.

"I'm looking every day, Auntie. You know these are hard times."

She fussed to herself for a few moments and then dribbled a little tobacco juice into her spit can.

"These ain't hard times. You just soft, that's what. You want to know hard times, you should have lived my life. I was born a slave. You ain't got no idea what that means. You been free your whole blamed life. You never picked cotton—"

"Neither did you, Auntie. Our family left Alabama as soon as the War Between the States ended."

I knew I shouldn't be talking back, not when she was giving me shelter, but I could only take so much.

Auntie pinched a bit of snuff and stuffed it between her lower lip and gum.

"Well, I seen cotton picked, and they had cuts all over they hands," she said. "And they backs was all bent up from dragging them heavy bags, and it was hotter than blazes."

"I don't see what that has to do with this here Depression," I said. "That's the trouble I'm living through, that's all I'm saying."

It would have been easier to dam the Mississippi than to stop Aunt Naomi once she got going good. I sat back and tried to think about something else while she carried on about Wall Street, the government, those blamed politicians, the white man, the price of bread and milk, how far she had to walk for groceries, her bunions, her shoes, *my* shoes, my no-count clothes, original sin, Adam and Eve, and why the Garden of Eden must have been in Africa.

The longer she ranted, the more she began to shake

her fist at me, at the world, at Heaven. When she did, it set
her bosoms to swinging inside her raggedy dress. Aunt
Naomi was somewhere north of seventy and her bust had
drooped south of her waistline, so it looked like a couple
of cantaloupes rocking back and forth in there. Plus the
tobacco-stained teeth and her hair so thin you could see
that mahogany scalp gleaming underneath. She looked
a fright and most of the kids in the neighborhood were
scared of her, called her a witch woman.

Not to her face.

All in all, though, she was a good woman and the
closest thing to a grandma I was ever going to have. She
raised my mama right beside her own children when
my grandma died young, so. And she did it without all
that much help from any of her three husbands. At least
to hear her tell it.

I've always wondered how she outlived three men. Did
she talk them to death? Well, that's neither here nor there.
She worked hard for seventy years, taking in laundry,
waiting tables, doing handwork. When husband number
three passed he left her this small house and a military
pension. She put down roots in Watts and meant to die
there.

But so help me, I wasn't going to.

~~~

I'D BEEN ON my own since I was fifteen. I left Virginia
for New York City in 1917, just as the United States got
involved in the war. That was when I first began to pass
for white, lost in the big city as I was.

New York was flooded with people passing through.
Soldiers getting ready to ship out and flocks of young
gals who thought they ought to treat those boys right

before they went and got themselves shot. Like it was their patriotic duty or something. The press called them "charity girls."

You know how it is when you got too many silly girls mixed in with a lot of young men ready for action. The plague of venereal disease that broke out was of Bibilical proportion. The gummint decided the best thing to do was to lock all them girls up, give them the cure so they wouldn't go spreading their sickness to decent folk. They put near thirty thousand of them into bobwire camps. I heard stories about how they were treated inside there that made my hair stand up.

I wasn't going to be one those idjits, giving it away for free and getting a dose in return. I wanted to find customers with extra folding money, men who needed some variety and relief from their frumpy housewives.

I admit I made plenty of mistakes, but I also made plenty of money as a working girl in New York. I was good at saving and smart at keeping hold of it.

I cut a deal with a Raines Law hotel, one of those places that was allowed to serve liquor seven days of the week as long as they also dished up sandwiches and rented bedrooms. This let everyone pretend the place was actually a hotel and not just a bar getting around the blue law that banned alcohol sales on Sunday.

I gave the bartender a split for any customer he sent up to my room, and I always made sure to call down for some extra drinks while I had a john with me. That way we both made a little extra.

You'd have thought that Prohibition coming in 1920 would have put a stop to all that, but it did no such thing. It just meant me and the hotel owner had to give the cops a bigger taste. That strengthened my feelings against the men in blue. The law had always been hard on my family and now they were making my life harder, too.

By the time I was twenty-one I had me two thousand dollars. I'd also had about all I wanted of the big city. I craved something simple and quiet, so I quit the life and moved to a nice small town: Peony Springs, Massachusetts. Nobody knew me—the men folk there hadn't been to New York to sow their oats, what with Boston being so much closer.

I told the people in town I'd inherited some money and leased a store front on Main Street. I opened a diner, called it the All In Café—making a play on my last name of Alwyn. It took a while, but being located right across the street from the courthouse and near the police station, pretty soon I had a set of regular customers. Even made a profit most months.

I hadn't lost the knack for saving and I knew how to be frugal. Three years later I was able to take out a mortgage and buy the place. I put in new booths and a Formica counter, plus one of them Italian coffee making machines I'd come to love in New York. When I fired it up in the morning you could smell the coffee two blocks away.

Now all this time I hadn't been seeing anyone, not a single solitary date. After six years in the business I'd pretty much had my fill of men. Well, you know how it is: If a woman keeps to herself like that, then a different kind of talk starts up. I did my best to ignore it.

But after a while I came to admire the local constable, a man they called Marshal Lawe. Most mornings he came in at six a.m., just as I opened. Wanted to get an early cuppa and some eggs with toast and sausage. Didn't try to get it free, neither, the way most police would. And he was always polite, didn't try to grab at me when I served him, like some I could mention. I noticed that when he was there the other customers behaved themselves better, too.

I began to change my mind about cops.

He said he'd never tasted eggs as good as the way I done 'em.

"What's your secret, Gladys?"

I must have given him a funny look. I had a list of secrets as long as my arm.

"You're too young to know how to cook this good," said Marshal.

"You don't know how old I am. I could be an old lady for all you know."

He laughed, shook his head, and gave me a look. I got all flushed.

"All right," I said, "I'll tell you the big secret, though it ain't that big. I cook that sausage first, then I scramble your eggs in the sausage grease, add just a little bit of salt and pepper with a dash of cayenne."

"I knew something was waking up my taste buds."

It was like that. Just friendly on his part. Well, maybe a tad flirtatious. I began to have thoughts about what life might be like as a married woman.

Besides, I did know how to cook.

~~~

HE AND I went through a bad time together.* It was in 1929 when our little town had a couple of murders, in a place that hadn't seen a killing in thirty years. The KKK lynched an Eye-tie, then somebody did away with the head of the Klan. And my colored

*In *Blood Harvest* (2008) Capital Crime Press

dishwasher disappeared right at the same time that a little white girl name of Jackie Sue Palmer went missing. I have to tell you I was scared, just plain scared.

Because no one in town knew that the colored dishwasher was my cousin, Darnell. And that I'd given him a job when he was straight out of prison, trying to get him away from his old friends who'd helped get him into trouble back in Virginia.

Lawe done his best to keep the town from going crazy. When her family got a letter telling as how she'd gone to Hollywood to become a movie star, he got it published in the local paper. He made sure that folks knew Darnell wasn't connected to the disappearance of Jackie Sue.

Still, everybody was stirred up and there was a lot of talk about how the immigrants were ruining our country, and the coloreds and the Catholics were getting way out of line. Lawe always spoke out against such sentiments. Told everyone he'd seen too much in the Great War to put any stock in that kind of nonsense, and the town folk ought to do the same.

After the troubles, Lawe spent more and more time over his late night supper at my diner and we'd talk until the last customers cleared out. We were seeing each other in a serious way. We began to think about a life together.

So how'd I end up in Los Angeles living with my great-aunt, you ask? Seems God has a sense of humor when you start making plans.

~~~

WHEN THE STOCK market crashed it didn't affect me all that much, but then the factory down river closed and about two dozen young women from our area lost their jobs. They came back to live at home on their family farms.

Each of those gals had been working at the mill to save up money for a down payment on a farm, so's they could marry the boy they was engaged to. Since there wasn't any work to be found in the town, either, those plans fell by the wayside.

The price of farm goods dropped through the floor. Crops that cost a dollar in seed, fertilizer, and labor to harvest only fetched thirty cents in the market.

One by one the farms and houses around town went into foreclosure. First one bank in town failed, then the other, wiping out most folks' savings. Of course, before my bank went under they sold my mortgage to a bigger bank in Boston.

No one had money to eat at some old diner; they had enough trouble buying groceries. I remember the price of milk went as low as a nickel for two quarts, though the milk looked like it might have been watered down some, with that bluish tint it had.

My boyfriend, who I called Petey in private but Marshal Lawe in public, had the misfortune to deliver eviction notices and announcements of goods auctioned to people he'd known all his life. He didn't like the job, and they resented him for doing his duty.

I missed one mortgage payment, and then another and another and then one day Petey was delivering a notice to me.

"Gladys, why didn't you tell me things were this bad? You know I would have helped you."

"Is that so, Marshal Lawe?" He winced when I called him that. "I don't believe that falls within your duty as an officer of the court."

"I have some savings, Gladys. We can get the diner back on—"

I cut him off. "I've never been beholden to a man in my live-long life. I'm not about to start now." You can see how I was: full of pride and self importance. "I got myself into this mess, so I'm going to have to bear the consequences."

He got a hurt look in his eyes that almost made me cry.

"I thought we were making plans, Gladys. We were going to make a life. Together."

"You don't want a bankrupt for a partner. It's a bad way to begin."

I reached out and took the foreclosure notice from his hand. He held on just a fraction of a second, and I could feel the shaking of his hand passing through the papers. Oh, God, if I could take that moment back.

He looked about to say something, but I spoke up first. "I ain't no charity case."

He turned on his heel and walked away.

~~~

IT TOOK ANOTHER two weeks to auction the fixtures from the restaurant and sell my few belongings. I had only ten dollars that I'd kept hid in a coffee can plus a small suitcase of clothes when I sat in front of the courthouse, waiting to take the bus to Boston. I hadn't asked him to, but Petey came to see me off.

"I know how you won't take charity, so I brought you this," he said.

He gave me a box of envelopes made out to his home address with stamps already affixed.

"Please write to me regular, let me know where you end

up," said Petey. "I need to hear you're doing all right."

"I'm going to stay with family. In Boston," I said. "See if I can find some work." It was a lie. I knew I'd work the streets until I had enough to buy train fare to my Aunt Naomi's in Los Angeles.

He reached into his coat pocket and brought out a smaller box, wrapped in gold foil.

"I know how much you like caramels." He tried to smile. "Don't eat them all at once. And think about me whenever you have one, okay?"

How sweet was that?

He had a tear in his eye and he turned away quick-like so I wouldn't see. There was a drop in my own as I watched him walk off down the street.

I was afraid I'd be thinking of him all the time.

Trick after trick.

three~
South Central Blues
July 1932

AFTER MY TUSSLE with Jones, the Hummingbird Café's owner, thought it best if I found other employment. I can't say as I blamed her.

"Now this here's your last week's pay, plus a little extra to help you get by until you find another spot. You a good cook. You be needin' a reference, have 'em call me on the telefoam. I tell 'em the trufe 'bout your cookin'."

"Thanks, Miz Patterson. I appreciate what you've done for me."

"You might check down to the Hotel Dunbar. They gots a restaurant and a jazz club and another diner next door."

I took her advice and soon enough I was short order cook at the Club Alabam, the hottest spot on the east side of town. Seems like good luck, right?

That's when I caught sight of my cousin Darnell. First time in three years, ever since he disappeared into the night back at Peony Springs.

He was carrying in a case of beer when we saw each other. He gave me a nod and I followed him out the back door of the club. He lit up a reefer and offered me some, but I shook my head no.

"What you doin' here, girl? I thought you loved yo' bushwah diner back there in Butthole, Massachusetts."

"That bushwah diner kept you fed and a roof over your head," I said.

"So why you here in the City of the Angels?" said Darnell. "You wanna get back in the life?" And he gave me such a knowing look I wanted to slap it off his face. But I held my temper, remembering the Hummingbird.

"My diner went bankrupt not so long after you disappeared. And I am not getting back in the life, Darnell. Now I've got a question or two. How is it I don't hear nothing either from you or about you for two, three years and then you pop up, clear across the entire United States, in the same restaurant where I'm working?"

"When I first come here, I stayed with Aunt Naomi until I gots me some cash. I found me some work close by where she live."

"You stayed with Aunt Naomi? I'm living with her right now in that tiny house of hers. She hasn't mentioned you at all."

"She know how to keep her mouf shut, if she know what good for her."

"Why are you talking about her like that? She's been nothing but good to us."

He took a long drag on his marijuana cigarette and held it for a good twenty seconds before he streamed the smoke from his nose.

"You lookin' good, babe. You done work your jelly roll round here, you make some serious money."

I turned in disgust and went back to the kitchen, pulled down the next order and started cooking. A few minutes later Darnell lugged in a case of whiskey. He stopped by to whisper a warning before he disappeared into the night.

"Best if you not let on you know who I am. Got it? And I won't be telling no one you my cuz, either. No sense givin' nobody a handle on us."

~~~

TWO WEEKS WENT by and I was beginning to relax. The work was hard, the pay was low, the nights were long, my spirit wasn't improving much, but I was saving a little bit every week after I helped buy Aunt Naomi's groceries. And then I got a postcard from Petey.

My land, I thought I'd faint from surprise. He had moved to Los Angeles and was doing cowboy work in the movies. He gave me the address and phone number of his hotel and told me he wanted to see me again.

I kept that postcard in my pocket and re-read it every so often. He didn't come right out and say it, but I got the feeling he'd followed me to the West Coast. If that were so why hadn't he written in more than six months? I admit it roiled up a lot of mixed feelings and my brain was at sixes and sevens as I cooked that night. If I hadn't been so distracted, I might have heard the commotion out front in time to duck out the back.

It was a raid and before I knew it the kitchen had three cops in it. I heard a lot of yelling from the customers out front. The cops lined all the kitchen help against one wall and began searching under the counters, in the cupboards and storage bins, then the food lockers.

One of the cops surreptitiously asked each of the men

if they had ten bucks. Those that did passed it to him, and he let them out the side door to the alley.

But then one of the other blue jackets found a joint in a coat pocket hanging on the peg by the door. The coat belonged to one of the busboys.

"Who owns this?" called out a big beefy cop, an Irish redneck from Georgia, by the look and sound of him.

Nobody said anything, so the cop just grabbed Isaiah, the first man who came to hand, and whacked him across the ribs with the flat of his billy club.

"I'm guessing it's yours, boy," said the cop. "Unless you have some information for me."

Isaiah was clutching his ribs and doubled over in pain, but he said nothing. The cop handed him the jacket and told him to put it on. Isaiah did and the coat was three sizes too big, with the cuffs hanging down below his finger tips.

"What's your name, boy?"

"Ize."

"Eyes?" The cop thwacked him a second time. "Don't be getting smart."

I couldn't keep quiet. "His name's Isaiah, but we all call him Ize for short."

The cop shot me a look of pure evil. "I'm not talking to you. What kind of white trash works for coloreds?" He grabbed Isaiah's chin and forced him to look up. "Well, Ize, it looks like we got us a situation here. You're about to be arrested for failure to cooperate with an officer in the course of an investigation, and for possession of an unlawful drug. Unless I get some answers real quick, I might have to add resisting arrest." He paused and got his face right close to Ize's. "We wouldn't want that, now would we?"

Right then another policeman brought in our other

busboy, Jacob, from the front room, pushing him face-first through the swinging doors. Jacob had a bloody nose and it had dripped across the front of his white apron. The whites were showing all around his eyes. His gaze darted all over the kitchen, hoping to find a friend, or a way out of this mess. His glance lit on Ize.

"Hey man! Why you wearing my jacket?"

All the cops in the kitchen turned to look at him, unable to believe their ears. I just rolled my eyes at the other cooks.

Jacob looked hangdog as they cuffed him and took him out to the squad car. I caught a glimpse through the door and saw two paddy wagons being filled with patrons of the club, the ones who wouldn't or couldn't pay the toll. A shout of excitement brought my attention back to the kitchen, as a detective came from the storeroom carrying half a case of whiskey.

"This gives us all we need for now, boys," the detective said to the cops. He winked at them as he said, "I may have dropped a few bottles as I was fetching this—maybe one for each of you."

And then I caught his eye. He handed the case to one of officers.

"Put this evidence in the van. I see I'm going to have to interrogate this witness personally." He pointed to another policeman. "Cuff the pinky and put her in the back of my car. I'll take her down to the station myself."

~~~

WE HADN'T DRIVEN more than six blocks, just enough for the others to lose sight of us, when he pulled his unmarked car over to the side of the road. We were in a dark patch between streetlights on Central. A car passed by now and then, its headlights briefly lighting up the interior. I watched as he went through my pocket-book.

"Not a smoker, huh? I like that in a woman. Shows some respect for her body." He found the single gold foil-wrapped caramel that I had saved as a reminder of Petey. "Got a sweet tooth, though." He unwrapped it and popped it in his mouth. He bit down, then muffled a curse. "Damn thing's stale." He spit it back into its wrapper and threw the whole mess out the window.

He pulled out my wallet, extracted the few bills I had and put them into his breast pocket. He rooted around some more and found the postcard from Petey.

"Here we go. Gladys Alwyn of 9517 Clovis. Down in Watts. You know, I've been tracking some problems down there. I'll just add this to my list of places to search in the warrant I'm getting."

Up till now I'd been keeping my mouth shut. Bitter experience had taught me that the less you told the police the better, but I couldn't let this pass.

"That's my great-aunt's home. She's putting me up until I save enough for a place of my own."

"Doesn't mean there isn't contraband hidden there."

"Please, sir, you'll scare an old lady near to death."

"I won't scare your auntie, if she isn't hiding anything." He turned around in his seat to look at me closely. I knew that look. He grabbed the collar of my blouse, letting his finger brush across my breast. "Besides, it'll give us something to talk about later on, won't it?"

He took me to the 77th Street Police Station where I was placed in a holding cell with two other women. They were colored streetwalkers, under the influence of something that had put them to sleep.

Opium, if I don't miss my guess. He went out front and I could hear him getting a judge on the phone, arranging a search warrant for a whole string of addresses. I overheard a woman with a voice as nasty as a Lilith address him as Detective Stone.

After an hour he came back to the holding cell and motioned me over to the bars. "I'll be back in a few hours."

"This isn't right. You can't hold me. I'm not under arrest."

"That's right, you're not. You are just waiting— cooperatively, I'd say—until I have a chance to interview you about the source of the contraband found at your place of employment."

"There were plenty of others to interview," I said.

He sniffed in dismissal and changed subjects. He motioned to the passed-out women. "See them? I wouldn't touch those pieces of trash if you paid me. But you, you I like. I'm going to be nice to you and you're going to be nice to me and everything's gonna be fine." He winked at me and left.

I waited until I heard him leave the station and then I began to scream as loud as I could.

In about thirty seconds the hookers began to wake up, surly as all get out. They yelled at me to stop the hollering, but I kept it up. By the time the desk sergeant got back to the cell I was quiet but the two women were threatening me and each other with a stream of cussing and screeching that wouldn't let up.

"Quiet down, you two, if you know what's good for you."

The hookers began cussing him now. One of them came over, stretched out her scrawny, pock-marked arm and tried to scratch him. He batted her hand away in irritation.

"What brought all this on?" he asked me, as the only one who was still coherent.

I nodded my bewilderment. "I don't know, but I do need to make my phone call."

The sergeant was seriously overweight. His gut put a strain on the buttons of his shirt that threatened to shoot them free at any second. The trip from the front desk back to the holding cell still had him puffing. He considered what I said and was shaking his head no, when one of the women spit at him, landing a streaky gob on his pant leg.

He gave the hookers a look that sent both of them scuttling for the wall farthest away from him.

He pulled out his key ring and let me out. When we got to the front, I fished out Petey's postcard and dialed his hotel, while the sergeant went to find something to clean his pants. The woman with the nasty voice kept a watchful eye on me, making sure I didn't steal the numbers off the telephone dial.

Fifteen rings later a clerk at the Kipling Hotel finally answered, wrote down my number, then went off to awaken Petey.

After five minutes of waiting on the line the sergeant came and took me back to the holding cell. The hookers had gone back to sleep. I huddled in a corner of a bunk that smelled about equal parts of urine and vomit, my arms wrapped around myself, and cried silently.

Petey called back fifteen minutes later. I was walked back to the front desk, and we got to talk for our three minutes before they marched me back to the holding tank. I could hear a lieutenant speaking on the phone with Petey as the sergeant locked me in again.

~~~

I DON'T KNOW how he did it, so now I guess I have to believe in miracles. I woke up about five in the morning as the sergeant was unlocking the cell door—and there was Petey. He smiled at me and held out his hand. I burst into tears.

"Let's go, Gladys. My car's out front."

I picked up my purse on the way out, getting a hard look from the nasty woman at the switchboard. I said nothing until we were in Petey's car and driving south, away from that slice of hell. Petey spoke first, his voice tight.

"Did that detective do anything to you?"

I shook my head no. Some of the tension went out of his face.

"How'd you do it?" I said. "How'd you get me out of there?"

"They had no reason to hold you."

"I told them that, but they wouldn't listen to me."

"Maybe it sounded more official coming from an ex-lawman." He smiled at me as we drove in the pre-dawn grayness. "You'll have to return for an interview if they ask, but that will be set up later."

"Petey—" I broke off unsure how to proceed. He took my hand and just held it, waiting. "Where are we going?"

"I thought you'd want to go home, clean up, let your aunt know you're all right."

"We need to stop someplace and talk before that."

He spotted an all night diner and pulled into its

six-stall parking lot. We went inside and I ordered coffee, but Petey wanted eggs and sausage and toast to go with his.

"Ask the cook to scramble the eggs in the sausage grease," said Petey. "And put a dash of cayenne on them, too."

The waitress rolled her eyes but made a note on her pad before she moseyed back to the kitchen to place our order.

"Old habits, I guess," said Petey, and I thanked him with a crooked smile.

"I need to tell you a couple of things before we get to my Great-Aunt Naomi's place."

The waitress came and poured our coffee, which was strong enough to clean radiators. We both added plenty of cream after the first sip.

"You don't owe me any explanations about last night. I got the story from the sergeant. You were in the wrong place at the wrong time, that's all."

"That's not what I'm talking about. It's something else. Did they tell you about the club where I was picked up?"

"I heard it was a jazz club," he said.

"Yes, and everyone who works there is Negro."

"Except—"

I shook my head to let him know I had more to say.

"You remember the dishwasher back at my diner, the one who run off?"

"Darnell? Sure, but what—"

"He's my cousin."

Petey sat back and considered this. "So your uncle married a colored woman?" He thought some more. "Or was it your aunt married a Negro?"

"Neither. My mother fell in love with a white man, but he ran off after she got pregnant."

He set his coffee cup down carefully, not looking at me, staring at the table top. I could see his mind spinning.

"I don't know what to say, Gladys. I never thought— You don't look—That explains—Well, I don't know what to say."

We sat silent for a good five minutes. The waitress brought our plates and Petey began to eat. He ate with a concentration on his food that made me want to scream. He still hadn't looked me in the face. Like he was afraid of what he'd see.

He finished his food, wiped his mouth carefully, then put his knife and fork on the plate, covered them with his napkin and got out his wallet. He signaled to the waitress to bring the check and when it came he pulled out three singles and put it over the check, almost a two-dollar tip.

"Dammit, Petey," I said, low and intense. "Will you look at me?"

He raised his face and stared into my eyes, tears brimming in his own.

Oh God, I felt ice water run from my heart to my crotch, like I'd fallen into a mountain stream.

And still he didn't speak.

I couldn't stand this.

"Thanks for getting me out of there. I'll be on my way."

He shook his head and put his hand on my arm.

"Then why don't you just leave?" I said. "I'm not that far from my aunt's. I'll find my own way home."

He tried to speak, I could see his throat working, but he couldn't get any words out. He put his face into his hands. He sat there for fifteen, twenty seconds.

Without looking up he said, "How long have we known each other? Eight years now? And how many of those years have I cared about you?"

"I'm sorry. I know it was wrong to deceive you."

He raised his head. "You thought so little of me that you wouldn't tell me this? Thought that I would let it come between us?"

And now I had nothing to say.

~~~

WE WERE SILENT until we were on the porch at Naomi's.

"You know it's still before seven, Gladys. Are we going to wake your aunt?"

"Actually she's my great-aunt. And don't worry, she's up by six every day to read the Bible and have her morning prayers."

"Is she Catholic?" he said.

Thinking back, I wonder if that would have been the last straw. He was already working under a heavy load.

"No. She's Pentecostal."

I got my keys from my purse, but he put his hand over mine before I put them into the lock.

"Back at breakfast, you said you had something else to tell me. I just realized you only told me one secret." His smile was a little tight, like it wasn't working right yet. "Not that it wasn't a big one."

"I believe I'll wait on the other till after you've met my great-aunt."

four~
Relative Blues
July 1932

WHEN I OPENED the door Aunt Naomi was standing just inside, her morning mug of tea in one hand. She took in Petey with a glance and then she looked hard at me.

"So. It's a shame, that what it is. A police bringing you home at the crack of dawn. You shaming this house, Gladys."

"He isn't the police, Aunt. He's my friend—"

"Don't you go sassing me, girl. I got eyes. I seen that police car soon as it pulled up. S'pose all our neighbors have, too. Goin' to be the talk of the neighborhood. I won't be able to hold my head up in church, listenin' to all them biddies tell me how they goin' to pray for my troubles. Then they be dropping by to 'miserate wif me, make me feel even worse than befoh. I'll have to serve 'em cake and coffee and be hospitable to some of them witches. I'm too old for this kinda nonsense anymoh—"

"Ma'am, I'm Petrarch Lawe. I'm sorry if my car is causing you any trouble. It's not a police car anymore.

You look close and you'll see the decals were sanded off. If you want me to park it someplace else, I'll be glad to move it." Petey took off his hat and offered his hand.

There aren't many things that ever shut Aunt Naomi up, but this was one of them. She took Petey's hand by reflex and let him shake her fingertips.

"I should have thought ahead about how it might look to the neighbors," said Petey. "You have an alleyway where I can park?"

"No, I don't. Never owned me a car, don't have a gay-rahj, either. It too late, anyhow. What's done is done. Everybody already saw a police bring my grand-niece home at dawn. Now they be talkin' and her reputation be shot. A police here on my porch—"

"Ma'am, I'm not a police officer—"

"Don't you be tellin' me any such rubbish. I know a police when I sees one."

I pushed on inside, pulling Petey along, and closed the door.

"We shouldn't be talking our business on the street, Aunt."

"Why he be saying he not a police? I seen a lifetime of police and he look just like all the rest of them."

It took a few false starts and about five minutes for Petey to explain that he once was a marshal, but had lost his job because of the Depression. And I told her how he'd rescued me from the 77th Street Police Station, after I'd been scooped up in a police raid on Club Alabam.

"Why a white man rescuin' a colored girl? That what I want to know."

"Aunt, you remember I told you about him before. This is Petey."

"Petey? I thought he said his name Petrarch."

"I don't use that too often, ma'am."

"Petey, hmmmm?"

Aunt Naomi looked back and forth from Petey to me for a long time, then motioned us to follow her. We passed through the postage stamp-sized parlor with its wingback chair set close by the picture window so she could watch the neighbors come and go. She made us sit down at the ball and claw table in her little dining room, amidst the Victorian wallpaper and chintz curtains. Petey inspected the family photos that lined one wall while she brought a kettle from the kitchen and poured us all mugs of tea.

"So you the one used to be called Marshal Lawe back in Massachusetts? I heard all about you. But I'm thinking you prob'ly didn't hear so much about me, that's what I'm thinking."

I blushed because it was the truth and because I was ashamed how I'd hid all this from Petey. Naomi saw and gave a mirthless laugh.

"The way she colored up tell me I hit that nail on the head." She looked at Petey. "She tell you her daddy white? And he run off when he got her mama with chile? That white boy was shiftless as the day was long and I told her mama so, but she wouldn't listen, no sir. And so she had her a little pinky baby and thought Gladys just too precious for words."

"Most mothers feel that way," said Petey, trying to take the sting out of it for my sake.

"All it do was make Gladys' life hell on earth, that what. Other colored peoples think Gladys and her mama stuck up, Gladys being so white."

"Please, Aunt Naomi. You've just met Petey. You shouldn't be putting all this on him. He had nothing to do with that."

"You think I can't see what goin' on between you two? I'm old, not blind." Naomi stood up abruptly. "Gladys, I want to talk to you in the other room. You 'scuse us, Mr. Lawe, all right?"

Petey stood up as we left the table, though I could see he was thinking we should just collect my goods and leave.

My aunt and I walked into my bedroom and she took my suitcase out of the closet, opened the chifforobe and began packing all my clothes.

"So you're throwing me out?" I said.

"Girl, there such a thing as going too far, and you've gone it. A white boy got yo' mama pregnant and it ruint her life. Now you fixin' to do the exact same thing. Well, I ain't going to have no part of it this time, nosirree. Not going to have you flaunt yo' white boyfriend around this here neighborhood. You going to move out of my house, girl."

"You're assuming a lot, Aunt Naomi. This isn't—"

"He get you with chile and he run off then I gots another mouf to feed and another shame on my family and I ain't havin' it."

"You've no cause to talk that way about Petey. He—"

She rolled her eyes toward the ceiling and clasped her hands together. "Help me Lawd! Gentle this wile chile. Bring her to Jesus."

She had raised her voice and I motioned her to hold it down.

"Don't you try and shush me," she said. "Not in my own house, no ma'am." She narrowed her eyes and hissed at me. "What about New Yawk? He knowabout—"

"Don't go starting on that," I said.

"Don't sass me. I seen the look in his eyes. And yours, too. And I ain't havin' it in my house."

She slammed the lid of my suitcase shut, jerked open the bedroom door, and marched into the dining room. I trailed behind her.

She put the suitcase down in front of Petey.

"I s'pose you heard some of that."

Petey just nodded.

Naomi had angry tears in her eyes. She pulled a little hanky out of the sleeve of her dress and blew her nose. "Well, you two think you so smart, you ought to take a little vacation together."

"What are you talking about, Auntie?" I said.

"I know young folk and you two be doing the sinful thing. Well, you just go and do it someplace else." She paused and looked at Petey skeptically. "You think you know everything, I can see it. Why don't you take her to Eureka for a couple days? You see what life is really like."

"What's Eureka?" said Petey.

"Where the rich colored folk go to relax. They call it the Black Palm Springs. You go there and learn a few things." She spun to fix me with an angry glare. "You both need some learning. See how black and white mix. You just love-blind fools."

~~~

AUNT NAOMI WAS right. I had no idea such things existed.

Petey and I had talked things over as we drove to his hotel. We decided that a couple of days by ourselves was sensible.

"Do you want to visit this Eureka?" said Petey.

"I don't know. She never talked about it before. But she's always tried to do right by me."

"Then she still is. I just finished a job and I have some money saved up. This can give us a chance to catch up." He smiled at me. "And make some plans."

"They still owe me a week's pay at Club Alabam. We can stop by and pick it up."

"Might be a good idea to make yourself scarce there for a bit. That detective might be back, and I don't know if I can talk you out of 77th Street twice in two days."

So we went to his room and packed his suitcase. There were a lot of empty bottles lying around, as well as the rumpled evening clothes of someone taller than Petey. I made a face at the typical bachelor disorder of the room.

"It's not my mess. I learned to keep a neat kit when I was in the army," said Petey.

A tall bony Irishman stepped out of the bathroom, and beamed at us.

"Marhsal, 'tis good to see ye. And I take it this is the fair Gladys?"

Petey introduced us and they kidded back and forth a bit before Al turned and began throwing his clothes into a suitcase.

"I can see that the two of youse will be needing this hotel room now," said Al. "I'll see if there's another to be had for myself."

"Gladys and I are going away for a couple of days," said Petey. "When we come back we'll only be here until we can find someplace more permanent."

"Say no more, lad. I don't want to be a fifth wheel."

Petey settled up the rent with Al and we took our leave.

We drove north from Los Angeles, crossing the San Fernando Valley toward the Newhall Pass. The road narrowed to just two lanes, though there were plenty of trucks, mostly loaded with produce, coming the other way from Bakersfield. Los Angeles is a big, hungry city.

The morning turned hot, rising into the nineties by 10:30. The San Fernando Valley was mostly farms, pretty and green. Lots of orange groves, the fruit ripening in the sun. The overheated citrus trees gave off a wonderful odor as we drove with the windows down, the wind brushing through our hair.

Once we crossed into the Santa Clarita Valley, the landscape got more and more dry. There were no houses, no farms, just cattle ranches with sparse grazing, miles of bobwire fence, mountains on every horizon. The road stretched out ahead, straight as an arrow across the valley floor, pointed toward Fort Tejon. I'd heard my aunt say that the Union had raised volunteer regiments there during the Civil War.

We pulled into a gasoline station at Castaic Junction and asked for directions to Eureka, which drew a funny look from the man pumping gas into a pickup truck.

"You two are headed to Eureka?"

"Yeah," said Petey. "I was told there'd be a sign for the turnoff near here."

"You go down here about two miles and you'll find a sign pointing you to Val Verde. That's the road to follow."

"Is there another sign later on for Eureka?"

"The place has been called Val Verde since the last century. That is until about five years ago. Then some coloreds bought up the abandoned properties out there and built a resort, started calling the town Eureka."

"That's the place we're looking for."

"It's for their own kind, if you take my meaning," said the attendant. "The county never got around to changing the highway signs."

I began to do a slow burn, huffing and puffing some, but Petey just thanked the man for his help and put the car in gear.

We turned onto a single-lane road that wound its way into the arid hills, following signs that said Val Verde was seven miles further. We crossed the Santa Clara "River" but all I spied was a dry bed of sand and boulders. There were no houses, no towns, not even many of the California oaks anymore.

As our Ford breasted the top of the first range of hills everything changed. Ahead of us was a small valley, lush with greenery. We slowed down, the better to take in what we saw. It was an oasis in a desert setting. We descended into the shade-covered lane that ran beneath the cottonwoods and live oaks

We came to the center of a small town and found a country store, with three ancient colored men sitting on its covered porch, rocking. There was a checkerboard between two of them, but neither seemed to be paying attention to the game. The men all looked at Petey's former police car with some suspicion. He pulled to a stop and the suspicion turned to hostility when they saw the color of his skin.

"I'll go get us some soda pop and find out where the hotel is," said Petey, but I could tell he was a little surprised at the anger in the men's eyes.

"You ought to let me handle this," I said.

Petey looked at me, unhappy, but nodded.

As I passed into the shade of the porch, one of the old Negroes said to me, "So you tryin' to pass, eh? Why you bringing your white boyfriend out here? This no place for a peckerwood."

I didn't reply, went inside, purchased the drinks, and got directions. I also bought a little map of the town.

As I went outside the same old man pointed at the car and said, "Ain't no call to be bringing no white police out here. We do just fine wif no police, just colored folk living peaceful."

"That's all we want, a peaceful life."

"You a dad-blame ninny, girl."

I walked over to the bottle opener that was nailed to the porch rail and popped the lids off my bottles of Nehi. I got in the car and handed the grape soda to Petey, keeping the orange for myself.

"What did that man say to you?"

"It didn't signify. He's just an ignorant old man."

~~~

THERE WAS A crick that ran through the town and it had been dammed, creating a small lake with a swimming platform in the middle. There was a nice strand of sand, plenty of beach blankets and canvas chairs. At one end of the lake stood a two-story hotel, a neat white clapboard building with doors and shutters trimmed a deep forest green. A nice collection of Buicks and Cadillacs were parked out front.

And everywhere I looked there were dozens of colored men and women. Some were dressed like they'd just come from church, the men wearing suits and ties, fedoras on their heads. Their wives and daughters mostly wore light-colored dresses, wide-brimmed hats, and carried

BRANT RANDALL AND BRUCE COOK

fans which they moved in a sinuous motion, keeping a
breeze moving across their faces. The families walked
slowly around the boardwalk that bordered three sides
of the lake.

An even greater number of colored folk lay on the
beach in their bathing suits or sat in the shade of umbrel-
las, drinks at hand. The lake was full of young people
swimming, splashing, playing water games, laughing,
calling to one another.

It was beautiful and serene and happy and ten other
good things. It was like I was in another world.

In my whole life I had never seen that much Negro
skin exposed to the sun at the same time. It wasn't all the
same color. The tones ranged from café au lait through
bronze, copper, brown, mahogany, teak, to a black so
dark it had a navy blue tint to it. But none were as light
skinned as me, not one.

I thought of all the taunting I had received as a girl.
How I must think I was better than them, just because I
was lighter. In truth I hadn't thought any such thing, but
I found you couldn't argue that one.

We parked the car under the shade of a pepper tree
and watched through the windshield of the car for
minutes that stretched into an hour.

Once we saw a colored man walking with a blonde
woman. From the style of his clothes and the amount of
her makeup I decided he was a pimp taking a favorite
whore out for a treat. None of the other people spoke to
them or even acknowledged their presence.

Petey watched and smoked and tapped the cigarette
ash into his pop bottle. I could see his police training in
the way he made mental notes of what he was seeing.

After a long while he said, "What do you think? Shall we check into the hotel?"

"This isn't my world, Petey. And I don't think they'd let it be *our* world."

He turned to look at me, a long careful study. "Is your aunt right?"

"About what?"

"Being love-blind."

"She's just an angry old woman who has been treated bad too often in her life. But that doesn't give her the right to tell me how to live my life. Nobody asked me what color I wanted to be born."

Petey started the car and turned around, heading back to Los Angeles.

We didn't talk much.

five~
Landlady Blues
August 1932

THE HARD TRUTH is that neither Petey nor I could make up our minds. We talked about marriage. Three times.

The first time was when we went looking for our own place to live. Petey was sick of hotels and transient neighbors. He wanted a place where the same faces came by every day, maybe said hello, perhaps even smiled.

We went to an apartment house on Kingsley, not so far from the Kipling Hotel. The manager, a Mr. Beraru, was an immigrant from some east European country, yellow in the tooth, and hard of hearing. From his ears grew tufts of hair that hadn't been trimmed since the Coolidge administration. You'd have thought he'd be pleased to see a well-dressed couple who looked like they could pay the rent. Instead he gave us a jaundiced look.

"I don't like no hanky-panky," he said.

I was afraid he thought I was working—well, it doesn't matter what I thought, because Petey took offense right away.

"You've no call to talk to a lady like that."

"I'm talking to both of you. This is a family building. We got children here, widows too."

"What are you talking about?" said Petey. "All we want is to rent an apartment."

"You not married. I'm not blind. She no got a ring on her finger. We don't want no trouble in our building."

"We're not going to cause any trouble," said Petey.

"What? You telling me you married but you forgot to buy her ring? I don't believe."

And he slammed the door in our faces.

As we walked back to the car I said, "Well, should we?"

"Gladys, if we get married it's not going to be because of some buzzard like that."

"Really? What is it going to be because of?"

He didn't have an answer to that one.

Of course, neither did I.

~~~

THE NEXT TIME was just after Petey landed a full-time job working security for MGM Studio.

"What does working security mean? You going to wear a uniform, be a private policeman?"

"Nothing like that. I'm more of a troubleshooter. Break up disturbances, talk to local law enforcement if a star gets drunk in public, that sort of thing."

I didn't like the sound of it, but it was a real job. I was waitressing, trying to find a job as a cook, and our savings were just about dry. "I guess that sounds pretty nice," I said, trying to put a good face on it.

"But here's what it really means, Gladys. It means we could afford to get married."

He caught me by surprise. Not that I hadn't been think-ing about it, but I didn't know that he had, too.

He was uneasy at my silence. "I mean, if you would like to. I mean—well, you know what I mean."

"Is that supposed to be a proposal?"

"No. But I'll ask you for real, right now." Instead, he stuttered a bit and kind of ran out of steam.

"But you need to ask something else first. Is that it?"

I could see him steeling himself to it. "If we had a baby, would it be—"

"Do you want children?"

"I thought all women wanted children."

"I asked if you wanted them."

He shrugged. "Sometimes babies just happen, you know."

I gave him a long look, waiting for him to come out with it.

"I mean, how can you be so light, when I saw how dark your aunt was?"

"She's my great-aunt. She was born on a plantation, raised as a slave until the Emancipation. And her father was the foreman on that plantation, a white man. Her sister, my grandmother Ruth, had the same father. That's where we got the name Alwyn. He was killed in the Civil War. After the war, when the family moved away, my grandmother Ruth married a mulatto. She died giving birth to their little girl and that was my mother, Pearl. And my mother Pearl had a white boyfriend. But you already heard that part from Aunt Naomi."

"God almighty," said Petey, and let it rest at that.

"I've got cousins who are every shade you can think of. But the truth is I don't know exactly how our child would turn out. And the way you're asking

—100—

this, I'm not sure how you'd turn out, either."

That was the second time we talked about marriage and I was still holding back. I hadn't told him the rest of it.

~~~

THE NEXT DAY I was off from work. While Petey was at MGM I took the trolley down to visit Aunt Naomi. I told her I was seriously thinking about marriage and asked her what she thought would happen if we had children. She ranted about the sins of the mothers being visited on their children even unto the third generation, about the iniquity of slavery, about the injustice of racism, about the inequality of law, about the disappearance of the Negro race because of miscegenation.

I didn't even know she knew that word.

I told her I wanted my birth certificate, but she wouldn't tell me where it was. No one had ever told me the name of my father and I found I wanted to know it, see what I could discover about the man whose facial features I carried.

My aunt said she'd pray for guidance.

"It's not Sunday, Aunt. There'll be no service."

"This place always open."

And she knelt down right there on her Sears and Roebuck Persian carpet, her eyes closed, her hands raised, and began to pray in tongues. There was nothing for it but to kneel down beside her and wait it out.

Twenty minutes later she stopped. Her brow was wet and so were her eyes. She looked over at me, a sad smile on her face.

"Sometimes we pray for things and the answer is no."

So that's how it was going to be. I'd gotten me some fake identification when I lived in New York, changing my age and race so I could rent rooms and buy alcohol. I figured I could make do if we decided to get a license.

~~~

FOUR DAYS WENT by quietly. When we both had a day off at the same time we went house-hunting again and found a little bungalow courtyard. Eight one-bedroom cottages with bathroom and full kitchen, a back porch with room for a washing machine, and a parking space out back. The cottages all faced into a nice garden area with flagstone walks leading to the front door of each cottage.

Petey didn't approve, but I bought a plain brass ring that I slipped on before we knocked on the door of the manager. A small plaque read "I. Berger" beside the door of a larger unit, situated farthest from the street.

An elderly woman with frazzled gray hair and thick rimless spectacles answered the door. She had shrunk to something less than five feet and her old raglan-sleeved sweater was covered with cat hair. I could see at least two felines behind her and she held a kitten in her arms, which she petted without ceasing.

Miss Ilona, as she insisted we call her, had come from Russia before the Great War. She told us her entire history in a nonstop flow of narration as she showed us the unit that was for rent.

"These little houses—they're so krasivyj—beautiful—aren't they? They were built in 1915, just year before me and my husband came here from Saint Petersberg—may devil keep Czar!—though now I suppose communists make even worse pogroms than Cossacks—and those poor children gunned down by anarchists and that fiend Rasputin. Yes, these were built modern, electrical inside walls, not added later—and running water and flushing toilets."

She paused to pull the chain and show us that the toilet worked. We followed her as she demonstrated the faucet in the kitchen sink.

"What is the monthly rent?" began Petey, but he wasn't quick enough.

"And little door under sink, so you can put garbage without having to walk outside and catching your death. See how light switch is here by door? And we weren't here more than year before my Moishe got tuberculosis and got sicker and sicker. The living room is nice size and there's plenty of room in here for double bed if you don't have two separate singles. The last tenants painted it fresh only six months ago, but when Mr. Mayer lost his job he and missus moved back to New York and now they live with his sister and her family—you draw drapes with this rod, see?—and venetian blinds can open this way to let in sun in morning but give you privacy at night. You can get milkman to leave milk and cream and butter every morning and company that delivers is kosher, if that matters to you. Anyway there is a market down street and you can buy your milk and bread there if you wish. Mr. Mazzeo is Italian and gets very good produce every other day, and I buy from him myself, though he is a cash-only man, no credit."

"We both have steady jobs," I got in. "We won't need cred—"

"For that matter I, too, am a cash-only kind of person. I know rent is little high, but this is quality location. My late husband, God rest his soul, always said location was key to real estate, and he was right. I never have any trouble renting these units. Since his death this is my only source of income, so I have to manage carefully and find quality tenants, that's really important—what with me not having any children to take care of me and rest of my family lost to me in that Soviet Union and damned purges—"

"We'll take it," said Petey.

I stared at him in astonishment. We had said before we looked that we would make the decision together. That's why we waited until we had a mutual day off from work.

"That's nice, Mr. Lawe. It's fifteen dollars a month and ten-dollar deposit which I give back at end of six months if you still want to stay and I still want to have you for tenants and you pay rent always on time—I'll go and get agreement and my receipt book. Meanwhile, you two newlyweds can look around and decide where to put furniture."

"What makes you think we're newlyweds?" I said.

"Your ring slipped and there's no white skin underneath, so I know you just started wearing it. And besides I saw look in both your eyes when I showed you bedroom, and that's newlywed look if ever I saw one." This last as she was slipping out the door.

"God almighty," said Petey, and closed the door behind her. He dropped to one knee, took my hand, and looked up at me. "Gladys, will you marry me?"

I felt like I couldn't catch my breath.

"But what about if we have children?"

He shook his head. "Will you marry me?"

"Remember that other thing I needed to tell you?"

"Gladys, are you going to make me stay on my knee forever?"

I gulped. "You needed to know this before you asked me to marry you." I decided to just get it out in a rush and see what happened. "I was a prostitute in New York before I moved to Peony Springs."

He got up slowly and brushed off the dust from the knee of his pants.

"Are you ever going to answer my question?" he said.

I couldn't say anything the way my heart was pounding.

"I know about that, found out when you applied for the mortgage on the diner. Bank asked me if I knew someone to do a background check on you. The report came to me first. By that time I'd known you for three years in Peony Springs. You never broke the law, you never cheated anyone, you worked hard, you didn't carouse, you didn't drink. I decided not to pass on the fact of your two arrests in New York. I could see that wasn't you anymore. You were a different person."

"But my past—"

He gave me a look and I stopped talking. Then he said, slowly, "I fought in the trenches in France. I did things I don't care to ever think about again, things I'm ashamed of. I've tried to be a better man since then, to make up for it." He paused and took a breath.

"So, will you marry me or not?"

MISS ILONA'S
HOLLYWOOD SCRAPBOOK
PART II: *WILLIAM DESMOND TAYLOR*

HOLLYWOOD'S DAILY TATTLER

FAMED DIRECTOR FOUND DEAD!
--February 3, 1922

William Desmond Taylor, 49, former actor turned director, was found dead in his Hollywood home. A witness at the scene said he died of a single gunshot wound to his back.

Neighbors reported hearing the gunshot and several said they saw a young, dark-haired man leaving Taylor's house.

The Daily Tattler asks: Is there any connection to the ongoing Fatty Arbuckle scandal? Is it really just a coincidence that two directors from Paramount are involved in murder within five months?...

MARY MILES MINTER SOBS OVER TAYLOR'S CORPSE AT COUNTY MORGUE!

--February 4, 1922

Eyewitnesses at the Los Angeles County Morgue said that Mary Miles Minter, one of Hollywood's most beautiful young stars, asked to see the corpse of director William Desmond Taylor, referring to the deceased as her "mate."

When allowed to view the body, she broke down and sobbed. She had to be restrained and removed from the room after flinging herself across the corpse...

TAYLOR INQUEST REVEALS STARTLING DETAILS OF HIS SECRET LIFE!

--February 10, 1922

The man known as William Desmond Taylor was born in Ireland as William Cunningham Deane-Tanner. He came to the United States in 1890 and eventually found his way to the Broadway stage, using the name Cunningham Dean. He married the daughter of a wealthy stock broker and opened an antique furniture business as "Pete" Tanner. In 1908 he deserted his wife and daughter and surfaced in Hollywood as the actor William Desmond Taylor.

After becoming a director he helmed *Anne of Green Gables*, which was Mary

Miles Minter's first starring role. She was 17 at the time and the director 46, but they became lovers. Coded love letters from Minter were found hidden in Taylor's riding boots by police...

The Daily Tattler asks: Is there any truth to the rumor that Paramount security was called before the police were notified of the murder of one of the studio's top directors? And did they clean the house of bootleg liquor as well as all scandalous correspondence from Taylor's paramours, but missed MMM's because it was hidden?

BOTH MINTER AND MABEL NORMAND WERE AT TAYLOR'S HOME THE NIGHT OF THE MURDER!

--February 17, 1922

Was a love triangle behind the death of director William Desmond Taylor? Was the dark-haired young man—described by some witnesses as effeminate—seen leaving the death house actually a woman, a spurned lover? Whose pink lingerie was found in the director's nightstand?

Or was the night visitor Charlotte Shelby, mother of Mary Miles Minter, there to protect her daughter from the advances of a man old enough to be her father?

The Daily Tattler asks: When will Hollywood clean house of the moral decay and corruption that infests this marvelous industry? How much longer will the public pay to see films made by moral degenerates?

WILL HAYES APPOINTED HEAD OF MOTION PICTURE PRODUCERS AND DISTRIBUTORS ASSOCIATION!

--April 2, 1922

Former Postmaster General Will Hayes will head the newly formed board to censor Hollywood pictures, protecting public decency...

The Daily Tattler says, "It's about time!"

AL HAINE

"Until he is dead,
   do not yet call a man happy,
   but only lucky."
      —*Herodotus*

one~
Belfast and Beyond
1920

DEATH FOLLOWS ME wherever I am, and thus my life seems to be a series of departures.

Though I was sired in Antrim, I was sent off to boarding school in Belfast when Da died.

"Your father has left a small legacy," said my mam. "Ye will be educated at a decent school."

"But I don't want to be at school by meself. I want to stay with you and me sisters," said I.

"Don't be cheeky. This is what your father wanted for ye."

Mam thought the good Fathers at our local school were already after doing their duty by me, so I was shipped to a school for well-to-do boys, both Catholic and Protestant. I wasn't but twelve, a skinny puling lad. And with a name like Aloysius Lambert Joseph Haine, there was no doubt that I was Cat'lick.

I was to be educated, I was. And live far from home.

What an education it turned out to be. 'Tis true that the Proddies were happy to teach me lessons, ones I never forgot.

I learned to use my fists the first week. In the next months I learned to use guile.

Once I got my height I learned the sweetness of revenge. I ignored the advice of the good Fathers at Saint Martins, that bit about turning the other cheek.

And so passed four years of misery and edification.

~~~

I FINISHED MY schooling during what the Chinese call interesting times—by which I mean the Easter Uprising to establish a united Ireland as an independent socialist state. The uprising failed, as so many Irish enterprises do, but it left me with a yearning for a more egalitarian world, one rid of classes. Yes, I'd half a mind to join the Communist Party.

In early 1920 Eire fought once again to free herself from the tyranny of His Satanic Majesty, George the Fifth. It was a bloody period, full of treason and betrayal. During these Troubles—which led to my own trouble, best left unspoken—I found myself departing from Cork of a sudden. 'Twas but a week after Bloody Sunday that I was bound for New York, aboard a ship full of Europe's huddled masses, yearning to breathe free.

Seven days of pure affliction upon the sea that was, suffering the *mal de mer*.

By way of contrast it was a wondrous sight when Lady Liberty herself greeted us in New York Harbor.

Me and Michael Grogan, a crony from the IRA, stood in a building on Ellis Island cheek by jowl with a foreign-speaking horde. Hours and hours sweating in a queue with hundreds of culchies, looking like they'd just walked off the farm. Nothing to eat but poorly made sandwiches and lemonade, sold to us by sharp-eyed men from little wheeled carts, and at dear prices, too.

After an eternity I came before an official who stood behind a lectern. He never looked up from his ledger.

"What's your trade?" said this officious little bandy-legged man, standing there in his rumpled uniform.

Truth be known, I had none, but I knew that wasn't the right answer.

"Skilled machinist," I said, though the only machines I'd ever operated were a Thompson trench sweeper and an Enfield 303.

The functionary wrote it down without comment.

When they asked Michael his occupation, he hadn't the wit to answer so well.

"I'm an entertainer," said he.

"An entertainer?" said the bandy-legged man.

"Yes, I can both sing and dance."

He was moved into a different line, and I never saw him again.

I myself was questioned and examined and prodded and chalked and deloused until finally I was let loose upon the shore of Manhattan.

~~~

I HAD BUT five dollars in my pocket and a telephone number. The five dollars I was after winning in a game of chance with three boyos from County Monaghan. The telephone number was given me by Michael

Collins himself. It was my most prized possession.

"It's for the best that you leave Ireland," Michael had said. "But get in touch with these lads once you're in New York."

"How can I be thanking you?"

"Fell service needs to be rewarded, but I can't do it with the bloody Brits still in power."

The telephone number led me to a cadre of Irish patriots bent upon the liberation of the whole of Hibernia. Those good fellows gave me a place to sleep, a job to do, and a wee bar to brag about it in. It was the start of a fine and industrious time, five years of plenty.

As I soon found out, the local patriots felt the most direct way to fund the unification of Eire was to assist my mates in smuggling Seagrams to the thirsty millions in New York, Philadelphia, and Boston. I learned to drive a lorrie—or truck, as the Yanks call them— and run the back roads from Canada into the United States.

Though I carried a gun, I never had cause to use it when crossing the border. But once, as I passed through New York City, I was set upon by a group of Eye-ties who wanted to liberate my cargo for their own purposes. Though the Irish were after controlling the flow of potables since the beginning of Prohibition, the Italians wanted a piece of that pie for themselves and thought they might take it from the "potato-eaters."

I had slowed to a stop because of a stalled Buick roadster blocking the boulevard. I could see a man with his head under the bonnet, his rear end protruding. Comical, I thought it was. Two other men appeared to be interested onlookers. One of them turned to wave at me, or so I thought.

In truth it was a signal to attack my van. In a moment there were men on all sides of the lorrie, murther in their eyes.

The first of them tried to yank open the door. He called through the open window, holding a shotgun to his shoulder.

"Pull over, Paddy, and save your skin."

I pulled the Colt from beneath a newspaper on the seat next to me.

"I'll save me own skin, thank ye."

He took the bullet in his forehead.

When his body fell backwards onto the pavement, the others stared at it in disbelief. They began to fire their pistols at the lorrie's cab fast and furious. I put the vehicle in gear, ducked below the dashboard, and mashed the accelerator to the floor, smacking the rear end of their automobile as I passed by.

Somewhere in memory a bell tolled for my misplaced youth.

The death of Vito Pinto marked the end of my career in New York. I was told to get out of town, or it was the dirt nap I'd be taking.

For some time before I was hearing that there was a fine Irish community in Chicago, so it was to the Windy City that I made my way. And I grew to be happy there, gainfully employed as I came to be.

But it turned out I would now be taking leave of Chicago, keeping an eye out in case this time the banshees came calling for me.

two~
Chicago
12 July, 1932

THE THIRD TIME was the easiest. It was that fact which stirred in me the greatest grief. There was no question that Tubby was deserving of the .45 slugs, but he died with such a look of surprise on his face.

As for surprise, I myself was soon to discover that it was but a short trip from Chicago to a field of maize; from a bespoke suit made by a fine tailor to hand-me-down overalls; from drawing a nice salary and living large to carrying all my worldly goods wrapped in a kerchief.

I'm not one to ponder the workings of fate, but on this occasion I began to feel like a mere plaything of the gods. Perhaps I needed to mend my ways.

Or at least go to confession once upon a time.

~~~

TUBBY AND I worked collections on Chicago's South Side for the Valley Gang. In the eyes of some that meant we were also working for Al Capone, since he provided protection to our gang in return for a share of the profits.

And what was it we were collecting for? Beer. By the barrel and by the truckload. For every saloon, bar, and restaurant in more than half the city. Beer for the working man, beer for the working man's wife, beer for those celebrating a special occasion, beer for those down on their luck.

Beer for the Irish and the Germans, the Poles and Slovenians, the Italians and the Negroes.

And in certain quarters, beer for the working girls. Also their protectors, the Irish cops. I could never quite decide who were the bigger whores.

We collected on behalf of the bosses. When someone didn't pay on time, we helped them see the error of their ways. In return we lived very nicely indeed.

A Thursday night in summer it was, with a thirsty crowd busy drinking up the inventory. I checked the barrels on hand at Hogan's Bar and Saloon, totted up those newly delivered to the storeroom in back, and did my sums. I knew that the Valleys were owed one hundred sixteen dollars and thirty cents.

Tubby was out front, counting the till, and keeping an eye out for boys in blue. There was a new man, Mike O'Brien, on the cash register that night, Andrew Hogan being home with the ague. As I walked up to the two men, Mike turned to me and handed me an envelope stuffed with cash.

Tubby looked angry. "You pass the envelopes to me, you dumb mick, not my partner."

To be sure, Tubby was a kraut and not the most sensitive of lads. Both Mike and myself took offense to his slur against our race.

"You ought to keep a civil tongue in your head," said Mike.

Tubby was not one to stand for chaff. He backhanded Mike across the face. Mike went white with anger, murther in his eyes, and made a move for Tubby. I jumped behind him and pinned his arms to his side, pulling him away, knowing Tubby would kill him in a trice.

"Calm down, Mike, or tonight will be the night you die," said I, growling into his ear.

I was so busy trying to get Mike out of harm's way, I didn't notice that Tubby was after pulling his revolver. I heard Mike grunt and I looked up to see the gun aimed at O'Brien's chest.

"Watch where you point that pop gun, Tubby. If you shoot him it will pass through and hit myself as well."

Tubby was red in the face, a vein throbbing at his temple. "Give me that envelope, Al."

"You're making a lot of fuss about nothing," I said. "What's gotten into you?"

"Give it to me now."

I retrieved it from my coat pocket, but instead of handing it to him at once, I opened it. Fifty dollars and an invoice all typed up, but bearing my signature. I plucked out the invoice.

I reached around Mike and held the envelope out to Tubby.

"You're a dab hand at forging my signature," I said. "That's quite a discrepancy there, lad. And two separate packets. You were trying to make it look like I'm the one skimming, when after all it's you."

As Tubby reached forward to grab the money I pulled the .45 from my waistband, the motion hidden by Mike's body. I reached around the cashier.

Twice I fired. Tubby got off only the one shot before he died but it caught Mike in the jaw and sprayed blood across my face and shoulders.

All conversation stopped and every face turned our way. At least a hundred and fifty witnesses. It was so still that all in the room could hear Tubby's death rattle.

The bar cleared of patrons so fast it felt like a magic trick. The waiters disappeared into the kitchen. I knew that at the inquest all of them would only have "heard shots," busy as they were washing dishes.

So why did Tubby turn on our boss? Why did he bite the hand?

I picked up the telephone from behind the bar and dialed Terry Drugan, head of the Valley Gang. It wasn't Drugan that answered, but Dutch Carpenter. When I identified myself, he said:

"So not only were you skimming, but now you've gone and shot Tubby."

"I've never skimmed and you know it, Dutch. As for Tubby, 'twas he that drew first."

"You're a dead man, Haine."

"And how did you hear so soon that Tubby was hit? Who's the rat that was watching us?"

"You'll be burning in hell tonight," said Dutch and he slammed the receiver down.

I scooped the remaining cash from the register and ran from the saloon. Outside I sprinted to the river's edge and threw the fatal pistol into the Chicago. I cleaned the blood from my face and shoulders, ruining a fine silk handkerchief, which I also consigned to the murky depths.

three~
South of Chicago
12-13 July 1932

IN ENGLEWOOD STATION I purchased a ticket for Saint Louis on the next southbound train. It was departing in an hour, so I took a booth in the station restaurant to have a meal before boarding. I went into the facilities there and washed the fear sweat from my body, straightened my clothes, and combed my hair. I took the bills I had liberated from the register at Hogan's and stuffed most of them in my sock. I left twenty-three dollars in my wallet.

When I came out I saw two men waiting behind a pillar, watching the door of the diner. One of them was from Capone's gang and the other was a palooka I'd seen hanging on the fringes of the Valley Gang, hoping for a spot as an enforcer.

I ducked back into the restroom and saw there was a window that overlooked the alley. I pushed the trash can next to it, flipped it over, and used it as a step stool to get my body over the sill.

Outside I took off my suit coat and tie, rolled up my

sleeves, and pulled off my celluloid collar. I strolled over to the tracks as casually as I could, then dropped over the edge of the platform and walked twenty yards while ducking low and keeping out of sight. When I resurfaced, there was a crowd between myself and the hard guys.

I kept moving until I was out of the station proper, then hailed a taxicab. The cabbie dropped me at the edge of the city and I walked until I found an underpass, where the trains roared overhead. It was dusk now and the 'bos were lighting fires to cook their evening meals. I sidled up to a group of four men standing around a fifty-gallon drum full of flame. They looked up in suspicion.

"I wonder if any of ye gentlemen would care to trade clothes with meself?"

Suspicion turned to outright hostility. One man, his face covered in a week's worth of beard and a month of grime, said, "If you're looking for a gunsel, the faggots are down the tracks a hundred yards."

"You misunderstand me. I want to give ye this set of almost new clothes, the suit made by a respectable tailor. All I ask in return is your clothing. It's in the way of a simple disguise, which I am in need of."

A large outdoor laborer stared at me. I took him to be a farmhand who was after losing his place. He wore overalls, clodhopper boots, and a rough flannel plaid shirt. He gave my clothes an appraisal.

"I'll take you up on that, mister. We appear to be about the same size."

The others gave him a look as if he'd lost his senses.

"But just to make sure there ain't no funny stuff, you skin out of those duds first. When you're down to your BVDs I'll take off mine and swap with you."

"I can see you're a shrewd businessman, sir."

I tossed my coat over first, quickly followed by shirt and tie. I put my wallet and change on the ground and slipped the shoes off by standing on the heels. I put my sock-clad foot down on my cash while I got out of the trousers.

When they saw the knife strapped to my leg, the hobos tensed. Once I tossed pants and shoes to them and straightened up, they relaxed again.

The farmhand got out of his clothes and tossed them to me. The man had no underpants and his genitals hung halfway down his thigh. I caught all the other 'bos watching from the corner of their eyes, a little uneasy at the sight of this naked man.

Farmer gathered up my raiment, smiling like he'd picked the winning number today. He fingered the suit and shirt with appreciation before putting them on.

"Don't forget the boots, sir. I'll be riding shank's mare tonight," I said.

He smiled at that. "You're not from around here, that's for sure."

"What, the accent gave me away, did it?"

Once I had dressed and put my wallet in the front pocket of my overalls, I felt a bit safer, though a good deal less savory. I was guessing that the farmer was not after bathing in some time.

I pointed to a bindle on the ground next to another hobo.

"I'll give you a dollar for your gear and another for your shirt," I said.

He didn't raise an eyebrow. Just took off his shirt, handed me the stick and kerchief-wrapped bundle. I gave him two dollars. He actually smiled, revealing an abscess on his gum the size of a penny.

"It has been a pleasure doing business with you."

As I turned and walked into the gloaming I heard one of them say, "All right, boys. The drinks are on me tonight."

I thought I might walk down the highway toward Saint Louis and hitch a ride. I hiked for more than an hour, cars whizzing by me, my thumb out, but in my newly acquired clothes no passenger car would stop, myself looking so rough.

However when I held up a dollar bill, a lorrie carrying a load of hay pulled to the roadside. The driver took my dollar but wouldn't let me get in the cab.

"You're welcome to catch a ride back there with the hay," he said.

He wasn't saying so, but I saw that he feared I might be a highwayman. I tried one more time.

"It's a chill night to be riding in the wind with no jacket," I said.

"Just burrow in between the bales. It'll keep the wind off."

So burrow I did, and the wee beasties that abide in bales of hay found me to be delightful company, as well as a filling dinner.

Two hours later the lorrie stopped at a rural crossroads next to a field of maize. The night was humid and the maize smelled lush. The driver hollered to me out the driver's window.

"I'm going east from here," he said. "Jump down and catch the next truck toward Saint Lou."

I did as I was told, watching his taillight recede into the darkness. Sadly, no more trucks came by. After an hour of peering down the dark highway, I planted my rump a few feet back from the road amidst the corn rows.

I was tired and hungry, since I was saving the sandwich in my pack for the morrow. The boots I was after purchasing were broken and crumpled, so my feet were sore as gumboils.

Tomorrow looked bleak. Following behind there were men looking to shed my blood. Though I turned the problem over a dozen times, I could see no way to assert my innocence with the bosses.

The night grew brisk and the wind moaned amongst the stalks, the leaves making eldritch patterns against the face of the moon. I began to think I should have knifed the truck driver and taken his vehicle. I wondered if the fourth kill would be the easiest yet, and not sting my conscience at all.

I suppose it was near midnight when at last I dozed.

~~~

AT THE SOUND of tires on the gravel shoulder and the glare of headlights I jumped to my feet. The car was upon me before I could think and I danced to the side, like a matador dodging a bull. The car's wing mirror slapped my stick and kerchief to the ground as the automobile dove into the irrigation ditch at the edge of the field.

The car's engine raced, then was shut off. A door opened and shut, but I couldn't see a thing else.

Had Capone's men found me already?

It was only a single set of footsteps I heard coming my way, and finally I made out the figure of a man against the dim glow of the auto's taillights.

"That was a close one, brother," I said. "I thought I was after greeting the saints."

The man started, then struck a match.

"Say, I'm sorry I give you such a scare," he said. "I didn't expect to find a soul on the road this late at night."

By the matchlight I could see he was as rattled as I was. He took a shaky breath and introduced himself.

Mr. Lawe, indeed. I saw no harm in giving him my own name since I saw little reason to believe he'd have occasion to tell it to anyone. After an exchange of pleasantries he suggested that if I helped him get his car out of the ditch he'd give myself a ride to the next city.

Well, we struggled and strained and sweated for some time before admitting the car was well and truly stuck. He offered me a spot in the back seat to rest until daybreak, and I offered him half the sandwich I had in my pack.

We sat in his car and ate and smoked and talked until he said, "I'd love to chew the fat with you some more, but I'm dead tired. That's how come I almost run you down. Let's call it a night and we can sort things out in the morning."

'Twasn't long before Mr. Lawe was snoring like a bucksaw at work. I lay there, mulling things over, trying out different plans in my head. I thought of relieving Mr. Lawe of his auto and leaving himself by the side of the road, but 'twould be a surly trick.

No, I would do the square thing and let him live.

I wasn't sure, but I feared I might be developing a conscience.

Besides Lawe might prove useful.

four~
Route 66
14-16 July 1932

IT WAS NOT yet light, and my stomach was gnawing on my backbone. Last night's half sandwich had been better than none, but that's about all you could say for it.

I eased out of the car and wandered into the field of maize, searching for some ripe ears. I heard small creatures also abroad in the night, and wondered if any of them might be edible. Though how would I be catching them? In the dark I tripped over the remnant furrows and managed to fall face down upon some small squeaker who must have thought the heavens were raining flannel shirts.

While the sky brightened a bit I found the ripest maize ears I could and headed back for Lawe's car. Though the car was black, like all Fords, I saw lighter patches on the doors.

"Jaysus, Mary and Joseph!"

Lawe popped his head up like a jack-in-the-box.

"Ye didn't say you were the law," said I. "Ye only said your name was Lawe."

"I ain't a lawman now. Used to be, though. Look closer and you'll see the Potemkin County Marshal decals have been sanded off."

Lawe went on to tell me how he'd been given the car when he was sacked in some country bumpkin town. Someplace that had no crime and thus his services were no longer required. It sounded like baloney to me. It appeared he expected me to commiserate, so I told him I was sorry he was after losing his spot in paradise.

We broke our fast with the maize and the conversation moved on to politics and economics, two subjects I am always prepared to discuss. One never knows where one might meet another student of Marx and Lenin.

"You being a communist and all," said Lawe, "I suppose you just liberated these ears from the field."

"Property is theft, brother. I was but saving their souls from eternal damnation."

He gave me a sour look and took our leavings to bury in the drainage ditch. I found him to be a neat and organized man. Always put his belongings back in their proper spot. Kept his car clear of rubbish. He was as easy to read as a headline. I knew he was coming to a decision before he did, and so I wasn't surprised when he proposed sharing the driving chores.

Since he was on his way to Los Angeles and that was as far from Chicago as I could get without leaving the country, I fell in with his plans.

Sadly, Marshal—as I came to call him—was a lad without much conversation, and I had to supply enough for the both of us. Still, he was a good listener, and I appreciate that in a companion. I chatted of this and that as we made our way across the great emptiness that makes up so much of these United States.

When Marshal did speak, it was always of Los Angeles and the wonders to be found there. The more Marshal talked about Los Angeles, the better I liked it. I'd heard no reports of organized crime on the West Coast other than San Francisco and I was given to understand those were all Chinese gangs. Los Angeles was ripe for the picking for an enterprising individual such as myself.

As an added bonus, I knew that the fillum industry was full of Irish Americans. Those dancers James Cagney and Ruby Keeler. The cowboys John Wayne, William Hart, Ray Corrigan. The actors George Cohan, Pat O'Brien, Walter Brennan, Spencer Tracy, Walter Huston, Gracie Allen. The director John Ford.

If I couldn't charm my way into that crowd of Hibernians, I could always fall back on my skills with cards and the bones.

~~~

THERE WAS A bit of amusement in some forsaken crossroads in Oklahoma. Foss, I think it was called. After filling the petrol tank at a tiny gasoline station, Marshal had disposed himself for a nap in the back seat. I went in search of cigarettes, but had higher hopes of finding someone to sell me something liquid and illegal.

Both Saint Florian and Saint Cayetano were looking after me that night, for I discovered a smallish shed-roofed building with a wizened man sitting on its porch. His face had the look of a dried and sunburned apple and he smoked a pipe made of a corn cob and a hollow twig, emitting a noisome cloud. He looked me up and down, taking in my bedraggled clothing and pausing especially to gaze at my hair. I returned his regard.

"Say, feller, you're not from around here, are ye?" said he, without removing the pipe from his mouth.

"No, sir, I am not. I am a stranger in this desert, seeking to quench my thirst," said I, laying my finger aside my nose. "If ye know what I mean."

The old codger's face crumpled up and he pulled the pipe from his yawper. He bent forward at the waist and began to wheeze and gasp so much that I was afeared he was having a stroke. After some moments he straightened and I saw tears in his eyes. He'd only been having a laugh.

"Oh, feller, you talk right funny, but I do take your meaning. I b'lieve you'll find your heart's desire right through this door." And he threw it open for me, calling to someone inside. "Got a customer needs a quart of your best, Arvin."

A twin to the man on the porch came up from behind a counter with a fruit jar of some clear liquid. He put out his hand.

"Be two bits," he said

"For water? That's dear."

Arvin unscrewed the cap.

"Take a sniff. Finest corn likker you'll ever taste."

I held the open jar to my nose. It smelled powerful, and I gladly proffered my quarter. I took a cautious sip, letting it burn all the way down to my privates.

By Gor, these men knew their potables. I took a deeper draught and was about to leave when I heard a tenor voice from a back room.

"Daddy needs a new pair of shoes." This was followed by the distinctive rattle of the bones.

I poked my head through the doorway, discovering five fellows on their knees, throwing the dice up against a wall.

"Is that a friendly game you got going?" I said. "Might a traveler join in?"

The long and short of it was that I spent a fruitful thirty minutes upon my own knees, turning a few dollars into several. One loudmouth, a particular RF Bealmear, who would have been well-served to drink less when placing his bets, eventually put up his personal flask to cover a bet.

He lost and I raked in the winnings, which included said flask. As I collected it he began to hurl accusations of cheating.

One thing led to another, and soon I had made kindling of a chair and bedfellows of my playmates. The last one standing got behind me and put an elbow around my throat, squeezing hard. I let my knees go slack, making him think I had passed out and putting all my fourteen stone on his arms. As my hand came level with my shin, I scooped out the blade strapped there and plunged it into the yobbo's forearm.

He yowled fit to break an eardrum, but loosened his hold on my throat. I spun about and came to my feet with a nice uppercut that put him down for the count.

Deciding that discretion was the better part of valor, I made for the car at full tilt. I had the good old Fordor rolling afore Lawe came properly awake.

Ah, but it felt good to be up to deviltry. Made me feel alive.

~~~

CROSSING THE BROAD barrens of America was like living a dream from Salvador Dali. Oklahoma, Texas, New Mexico, Arizona. Desert, cacti, Indian reservations, diners made from railway cars, empty sky. We ate, we drove, we slept; we got lost, we passed through a painted desert; saw logs made of stone in a petrified forest.

When I saw those rock-hard trees I feared the tales of Sodom and Gomorrah might be true. Perhaps the Mormons were right in believing that one of the lost tribes of Israel had settled here.

If you haven't heard the story before—that is, if you lack the fine parochial education I received as a child—it seems that God sent an angel to spy out whether there were any of the righteous left in those two sin-filled cities. The only ones to be found were a man named Lot and his family. God determined to punish the rest of the citizens, but the angels told Lot, his wife, and children to get out of town quick, without looking back, or they would be turned into pillars of salt.

You know what it's like telling a woman something like that. No sooner had they hit the road than Lot's wife turned around to watch the cities burn.

By what I have always thought a curious coincidence, she *was* instantly turned into a pillar of salt.

Women.

All the while we walked amongst those stone trees the sun blazed down upon us fiercely.

And I swear by Saint Felix we fought off spiders the size of cats. Well, the size of rats at the least.

The fever dream came to its height somewhere in Arizona. We had need of water to fill the automobile's radiator. Marshal had as much persuasive power as a scarecrow, and when he had failed to secure the necessary,

I took matters into my own hands. I made for a porch and knocked up the residents. A young boy answered the door, and once I impressed upon him that I had need of speech with his father, the man himself was summoned.

Time slowed as a beefy Brit in a sleeveless vest, and sporting an outsized mustachio, came to the screen door. Despite the fact that he stood in the shade of his porch I could see his face turn a deep crimson.

Though I had last spied him across a barricade in Dublin in 1920, I would have known him anywhere, anytime.

"So it's you, Haine, you murthering mick," he said. "I thought I had put an ocean and most of a continent between you, me, and the memory of that day. Come to my door to slit my throat, too, I suppose."

"I never killed your brother, Sergeant," I said. "That was a lie then, and it's a lie now."

But in actuality, it was the truth then and always.

From within the house an unseen woman called out, "Who's at the door?"

"It's one of the Apostles," said the Sergeant.

"Don't blaspheme, Thomas!" screeched his missus. "I'm trying to raise the boy as a good Christian."

Thomas rolled his shoulders, like he was trying to shift a weight that was more than he could bear.

"You've no reason to say I was one of the Apostles," I said, keeping my voice mild.

"Your own mates informed on you, you piece of shite. I figured they put an end to you themselves, but I see you must have cut and run, like the coward you always were."

About this time the sergeant's lad came to stand behind his father.

"He's an Apostle?" said the boy. "This man knew Jesus?

"No, Billy. It's just a sacrilegious name given to a squad of assassins in Dublin," said his father.

Billy rolled his beady eyes between his father and myself.

"What's wrong, Dad? Why were you two yelling at each other?"

"This here's the barstard that killed your Uncle Ted, Billy," said Sergeant Wesley.

Billy's eyes widened and he shrank back a step.

"Shall I get your gun, Dad?"

I didn't wait for the answer. I made for the car.

Again I heard the faint echo of malignant gods cackling. Did Michael Collins know that Wesley had emigrated to the United States? And then I remembered: Michael was dead these ten years and more, killed by a Judas hand.

Had I a gun I'd have gone back and killed the sergeant, his harpy wife, and the snot-nosed runt.

five~
The Golden State
17 July 1932

AT LAST WE found our way to Los Angeles. Truly it was the City of the Angels. Though the shape of the landscape was no different than the arid regions we had crossed for a thousand miles, for some reason there was water here. And the water brought flowers and fruit trees and palms and grass and farms.

It was paradise. It was Ireland with sunshine added and more warmth, but without the humidity of the East or Midwest. Why had it taken me so long to make my way to the Pacific Coast?

Marshal and I found temporary rooms and got ourselves cleaned up. Industrious as the lawman was, he immediately went and looked for work. I knew he was down to his last few dollars and feeling anxious.

As for myself, I liked the idea that a nickel would take you anywhere the trolley lines ran. By a happy circumstance they ran out to the Culver City Kennel Club. I divided my remaining cash into two piles. With the first

I bought myself some cheap but serviceable pants, shirt, and shoes—not wishing to look like a hobo any longer. The second pile was to be my stake at the dog track.

The journey took an hour, with only one change of line. The morning was clear and bright, not a cloud in the sky. The ladies who embarked in Westlake Park wore their lightest cotton summer frocks sans camis, adding immensely to the scenery.

As the trolley turned south along Figueroa, I found that Los Angeles had folks of many darker hues, much like New York—Japanese, Chinese, Mexicans, and Negroes. I hoped that meant as much variety in restaurants. I was tired of Midwest steak and potatoes.

Soon enough I was paying my admission to the dog races. I purchased the daily racing sheet and chatted amiably with some of the other punters as we waited for the first race. One young ferret-faced man who introduced himself as Izzy was most anxious to persuade me of the value of his recommendations.

"Listen, Al, my tips always finish in the money," said he.

"If that's so, why aren't your shoes shined?" I said.

He gave me a look of great disgust, yet he persisted.

"My shine's got nothing to do with it," he said. "I have a busy schedule, getting this tip sheet run off the mimeograph at the crack of dawn."

"I'll tell you what. I'm going to watch the first race without your sheet before I chance my arm. I want to see the form of the dogs here on the West Coast. I'll find you before the second race goes off."

He snorted his disbelief and went after another mark. I turned to the ancient codger on my left, a man of few words and even fewer teeth.

"I see you have a dope sheet," I said. "Who'd you buy yours from?"

He looked at me for some time, his mouth working silently, as if he were uncertain he should share such inside information.

"Jimmy the Dip."

"You're having me on, now. His name is Jimmy the Dip?"

Codger gummed something invisible for a few moments, seemed about to speak, but thought better of it. He just nodded yes.

"Where I come from a dip is a pickpocket, you know yourself. Funny nickname for a race tout," said I.

Codger squinted as if the sun were in his eyes.

"Yep. He were one," said Codger. "No more."

"I was thinking that I'll buy a sheet from Izzy and we can compare notes for the later races. Is that all right by you?"

"Like Jimmy's picks better'n Izzy's," he said.

I decided I'd like to make the acquaintance of a man who'd been both a pickpocket and a tipster, so I asked the codger where I could find Jimmy. He pointed him out to me: a man in a cloth cap and plaid suit coat standing in the shade of the grandstands; a man with one arm, his empty sleeve pinned up so it wouldn't dangle.

Codger caught my glance.

"Cut it off," said Codger. "Paid him back."

"That's rough justice. In Ireland dipping wouldn't get you more than a year in gaol."

Codger ruminated on that one and then spat a stream of tobacco juice from the side of his mouth.

"Knew you talked funny."

I sought out Jimmy and made the silly sod happy

BRANT RANDALL AND BRUCE COOK

by pretending I thought he'd lost his limb in the Great War. We swapped war stories, both of us lying happily. At last they called the dogs to post and I found a spot along the rail.

I don't know if it's the climate, the pure ocean breezes, or the quality of the dog chow, but those canines could run. Unlike the tracks back home, they used a mechanical rabbit, so there was no frenzy of killing at the end. I thought that precious, but put it down to the American aversion to blood sports.

True to my word I sought out Izzy and bought his racing form, then compared notes with the codger. I ran through the odds on the entries for the next race, then went down to see the dogs in person. There was one likely beast, fierce of eye and of sound wind. When I saw that he was named after an Irish hero, Finn MacCool, I knew I had my choice.

I was at the pari-mutuel window staking ten dollars from the stash in my sock when Jimmy came up behind me.

"That's a fool's bet, Al. It's gonna be Blitzen by two lengths." He tugged at his earlobe. "I've got inside dope."

I looked at him and saw he was serious as a toothache. I handed another five to the cashier and said,

"Put five on Blitzen as well." I turned back to Jimmy. "If you're right, I'll cover both bets at current odds, even if I give you a taste. But if I'm right, I'll have multiplied my stake by ten."

Jimmy had that glow in his eyes that said he lived for the score. He was a con man if ever I'd met one. Short cons, if he was working the track.

We joined the codger trackside to watch the race. He had a two-dollar bet on Blitzen and it must have been his life savings from the way he sweated. As the race time came closer, he bit off another big chew of tobacco and began to gnaw it vigorously. I made sure to stand to his left after having seen him spit to the right several times.

When the dogs were let loose the three of us all strained forward, the better to see the finish. A great roar went up as Blitzen pulled out in front and Codger pounded on the railing, alternately spitting and exhorting his dog to greater effort.

But at the last turn Finn MacCool came around the edge of the pack and moved closer to Blitzen, until he was just off his haunch. I borrowed Jimmy's binoculars just in time to see Finn nip Blitzen's tail. The lead dog snapped his head around to see what was deviling him, and in a flash MacCool was ahead.

They finished one-two. Codger was going to get his two dollars back with twenty-five cents to spare.

I, on the other hand, was going to collect one hundred and sixteen precious simoleons.

I treated both Jimmy and Codger to cigars I bought from a passing cigarette girl, a lovely lass with excellent lung development, making it a treat to retrieve smoking material from the tray about her neck.

"All that's needed to make it a perfect day is something to wet the whistle," I said. "I'll stand you a round if you can point me in the right direction."

Codger licked his lips, but offered no advice. Jimmy, however, came through.

"I know of a place where we might find something to drink, even bend an elbow for a bit," said Jimmy.

Somehow I had sensed he would.

~~~

WE REPAIRED TO an unmarked gin mill a few blocks from the track. Along the way I spotted a bespoke tailor and made a note to myself to return.

Jimmy knew the barkeep by name, just signaled to him to set us up. Jimmy and I took the inside seats at the booth, Codger kind of perched at the edge, looking uncomfortable. A good-looking colleen in a peasant blouse came over with a tray and we were served a beer with Seagrams chasers.

Codger poured the beer down his throat in an acrobatic manner, then gulped his shot of whiskey. He doffed his cap to me in thanks and made for the door.

I took a long swallow of the beer. 'Twasn't Guiness, but it wasn't bad.

"What's the name of this brew?" I said. "I've never tasted it before."

Jimmy smiled. "Brew 102. Made here in Los Angeles, Eastside Brewery."

"How do they get away with that? I thought Prohibition was the law for the whole country."

"Rather than put the brewery out of business, they let them make the beer, then remove the alcohol. What's left is near beer," said Jimmy. "The grain alcohol is sold to the medical industry."

I got the picture. "But there's always some of the beer that gets lost along the way, spillage and such."

"And the lost beer finds its way here," he said.

"Who runs it? The Eye-ties? The Jews?" I smiled. "The Irish?"

"This isn't Chicago, Al. No need for organized crime. It's just business."

"No mob has moved in?" I was having a hard time

Tommy Gun Tango

believing my luck. "Surely someone has to arrange things with the boys in blue."

"The coppers do drink up some of the profit." Jimmy snickered. "But it's like they say. In California there's enough sunshine for everyone."

~~~

THE NEXT DAY my speculations at the track proved fruitful again. The tailor had completed my new clothes. I'd had a haircut and soaked away my cares at the Bimini in Hollywood, a Turkish bath of varied delights. The back room hosted an ongoing game of craps which saw the sun neither rise nor set. My wallet was fattened considerably.

In short, I was my old self again. All that was needed was female companionship. I asked the night man at the Kipling where a man might find a little action.

George, as his name might have been, gave me directions.

"Take the trolley up past Chinatown. Get off at Olvera Street, go into the Plaza."

He stopped and gazed at me, sizing me up.

"What?" I said.

"How much action you looking for?"

"Everything that is offered."

He nodded, resolving something in his mind.

"Look for the firehouse," he said. "Just to one side is a small street, Nigger Alley."

"Truly? That's the name?"

"It's got some Mex name, means the same thing. You can find anything you want there."

I doubted that. It must have shown on my face.

"Street used to be wall-to-wall saloons, gambling

—139—

houses, dance halls, opium dens, and whore cribs, with a band in every joint. The Chinks ran it. Couple of factions, they call themselves tongs, got to fighting. Killed a white man in the crossfire. My granddad told me about the riot that followed. The murder riled up the Anglos and the Latins. By the end of the day there was three spots with yellow bodies a-hangin'."

"You say there were lynching's here in the City of the Angels?" I was surprised, thinking that was more of a Southern thing.

"That caused the alley to clean up some. But you can still get just about anything there is to be got."

~~~

I GOT OFF the Red Car about ten, hearing the church bells ringing out the hour as I walked into the Plaza. I spotted the firehouse and made for the alley next to it.

It was a street that could have been found in Hell's Kitchen or Chicago's South Side. I could smell the gin and hear the jazz from fifty yards.

A small sign proclaimed the first business was owned by Moe. It held the promise of refreshment, so I went inside. To my left, a quartet of Negroes on a bandstand the size of a handkerchief whispered a raspy version of "Minnie the Moocher."

I made my way to the bar, a long slab of mahogany that glowed burgundy red, polished smooth by the erratic ministrations of the barman's rag and myriads of elbows, then scarred with the slug-shaped burns of a thousand abandoned cigarettes. I'd bent an arm at the twin of this bar in many a city, from Galway to Antrim, New York to Chicago.

It felt like home.

TOMMY GUN TANGO

I had a Brew 102, followed by four more and a jigger of Jamesons. I felt the burdens of the day begin to lift. Chicago and the mob were far away.

One more draft of the water of life and I found that I happened to be in fine voice that night. I decided I would accompany the Negro quartet and made my way to the bandstand to offer my services.

"Can ye sing the Rose of Tralee?" I extended a ten-dollar bill to the one I took to be their leader.

"Come again, sir?" said the Negro, giving me a bright smile and making the folding money disappear.

"Rosatralee." Even to my own ears there was some slight slurring to my speech.

"Do ya mean Sweet Rosie O'Grady?" he said.

"Not the same woman at all."

"Sorry, boss."

"Well, then. Let's sing 'The Wearin of the Green'."

"I don't believe I know it," he said.

"Then ye must be knowing 'Bold Fenian Men'."

"Never heard of that one, no sir."

"How could ye never have heard of 'Bold Fenian Men'?"

He shook his head, still smiling, but less brightly. "I be knowing 'Danny Boy,' if you like."

"I thought you were musicians," said I, "but I fear you are mere minstrels." In hindsight I can see that this was not a politic remark. The Negro looked toward the bar and soon a large man had hold of my collar and the seat of my pants.

Normally I get along well with bouncers, tipping them liberally and causing no trouble. This particular bouncer was somewhat taller than myself and twice as broad. His small, unfriendly eyes were shaded by a single

—141—

eyebrow of unusual depth and wildness, a veritable zareba of eye-hair.

A foolish man would have called him fat, but in truth it was all solid muscle in his barrel-shaped body. I decided I would befriend him as he frog-marched me toward the door.

"Hey!" I began.

"Shhhhhhhh," said he.

"Gah queschun." I was having trouble with my speech. "How? You getsofat?"

He knitted his single brow. It looked as if a large caterpillar was inching its way across his forehead.

"Mmmmmmm?" he enquired.

"Fat," I clarified. "Fat."

"Rrrrrrrrrrrrrrr!" he retorted, as we picked up speed. Apparently he had no vowels. I pointed this out.

"Ya haven enny vowels, sir."

At this point we hit the saloon doors and parted company, myself passing into the fresh night air of the alley. I lost my balance and tumbled to the macadam, barking my knees and the palm of my hand.

I stayed there some time, down upon all fours, contemplating my plight. What I needed was a wash up and a drink, though not in that order. Arising with some difficulty, I bypassed Moe's and entered the next establishment, which was nameless.

My problem had been the Brew 102, I saw, so I switched to the house poteen. It tasted of peppermint and smelled of sulphur, but it had a presence that denied refusal. I drank two quickly then called for a third shot with which to clean my wounded hand and knees.

The barkeep objected to me pulling my pant legs up to my thigh, the better to see my knees. Two bouncers, each smaller than the man at Moe's but large enough all the same, escorted me back to the alley. They looked enough alike they might have been brothers. The both of them rushed me across the macadam and propped me against an adobe wall, still warm from the day's sun.

"Don't try to get back in, iffen you know what's good fer ya," said one of them.

"Where did ye learn to speak? You sound like a culchie."

The second man pressed my face against the adobe. Hard. "I'd shut my pie hole, iffen I was you."

I shut it. They released my arms and I heard them walk away.

The warmth felt good against my forehead and I must have dozed there for some time. I was awakened by a tugging at my pocket.

I cracked my eyes open to see two hobos fussing about my person.

"Wallet must be in some other pocket," said the first 'bo, a man cadaverously thin.

"Maybe someone already skinned him," said the second, who was better fed but had a squint in one eye. "Let's take his clothes. They'll fetch us a few bucks." He had a strong Okie accent.

"Here," I said, "Didn't your mum teach you right from wrong?" I tried to get to my feet, but the second 'bo pushed me back to the ground.

Skinny looked surprised that I was awake. "I thought those mickeys were supposed to leave 'em down for the count," he said to his companion.

"Who you calling a mick?" said I.

"Shuddup." And with that the first 'bo rapped me alongside the head.

My head was already tender from the drink, the efficiency of the first bouncer, and the roughness of the adobe wall. Still, the pain helped clear my mind and I gathered myself together. I rose to my feet and landed a nice tight jab on Skinny's nose, causing it to gush crimson. He cried out in anguish, then came at me, pummeling my ribs with a flurry of blows.

I got my hands around his throat and began to squeeze, determined to take the bastard down.

Squint-eye stepped behind me and jerked my suit coat down around my shoulders, pinning my arms to my sides. He put both hands together and gave me a poleax chop to the back of my head, knocking me to my knees. He got his arm around my neck and squeezed my throat in the crook of his elbow.

Even with my arms straitjacketed by my coat, I was able to get a hand up my pant leg and pull out my shiv. As the first 'bo moved in close to rifle my pockets I brought the blade up into his crotch and twisted.

He didn't let out a sound, but his eyes bulged, and his lips worked as he tried to scream.

Being choked as I was, I couldn't reach behind me, so I snapped my head back, straight into the teeth of the man in back of me. He gave out a whoof and fell away. I dropped onto my side and rolled twice to the left. The buttons to my suit jacket popped and I was able to shrug it back onto my shoulders and get to my feet.

The second 'bo bum rushed me. He never saw my knife, but it slid between his ribs with a silken whisper, piercing his heart. His momentum crashed the both of us into the adobe, but I slung him to the side, pulling back my blade. He was dead in seconds.

I walked over to the first 'bo who had crumpled to

the ground, cradling his mangled gonads, whimpering a plea to the Virgin to save his balls.

Pitiful.

I grabbed him by the hair, jerking his head up. "Stop your crying and be a man." I pulled the blade across his larynx quick-like.

God, but didn't I feel alive! I was born again. I knew that tomorrow I'd sink into a despair as dark and sweet as sacramental wine, but tonight I was drunk on survival.

The bells of the nearby Catholic church tolled two a.m. I made my way to the fountain in the plaza and baptized myself, getting rid of the gore on my clothes, then took the trolley home again, jiggety-jig.

six~
Great Expectations
20 July 1932

IT TOOK A couple of days to recover from my venture into Chinatown. I had my suit repaired and ordered another, one with a quiet pinstripe of red amongst the navy blue. I passed several profitable afternoons at the Kennel Club and from there found my way to the Cotton Club, which was only half a mile away. There I could spend my winnings while dining well and listening to hot jazz.

The club was huge, the size of a warehouse. There were easily fifty tables clustered around the main dance floor, and there were two more dance floors besides. The ceiling was draped in huge swathes of colorful fabric with bright stripes, so that it felt as if you were in some gigantic tent.

They did a live radio broadcast every night from the Cotton. Louis Armstrong on trumpet and Lionel Hampton drumming like a madman or playing like lightning on the vibraphone. When they went off the ether, the Cocoanut Grove began their broadcast with the Bing Crosby Trio. Later Bing would come in to relax and listen to the band until they played "Goodnight Sweetheart."

Most nights there were dance contests. I saw Joan Crawford take home a trophy, though I thought it had to have been rigged, clumsy as she was on her feet. Her partners must have kept the podiatrist busy. I myself entered the terpsichorean competition a few times. While I never won, I did place and show.

Between sets I would go outside to smoke. Armstrong and the band were usually there smoking gage, and they pointed out who I could buy marijuana from, a buck named Darnell.

"I understand you're the man," I said. He rolled his eyes and said nothing. "I'm looking to buy."

"Why you talking to me?" said Darnell. He moved so that the streetlight was behind him and shining into my face. "I don't know you."

"Louis said you're the man. The man who can."

"The man who can what?"

"Sell me half an ounce of your finest hemp."

"Louis said that?"

I nodded and the transaction proceeded. A couple of men in lightweight suits and fedoras came around the corner. They were off-duty cops or I'm a beefeater. Darnell glanced at them as he pocketed my cash. Once I had the weed in my hands, Darnell stepped back into the shadows.

"Bring the law down on me and you gon' be sorry," he said. "Big carrot top like you ain't so hard to find."

"Don't be that way. I thought we were going to be friends," I said.

Darnell hissed, maybe a laugh, maybe a threat. At any rate he shimmied into an alley and disappeared.

I waited until the flatfoots passed into the parking

lot and drove off before charging my pipe. I had a nice meerschaum with a curved stem I'd taken off a mark at my last game of craps. It mellowed the smoke—any smoke—very well indeed. The gage calmed the fever brought on by dancing and drinking beneath that big striped roof.

I'll never forget the night Cab Calloway came by and Armstrong coaxed him onto the dais. That man could howl down the moon. The whole joint was jumping and jiving as he hi-di-hi-hi-ed from the stage

And sometimes, if the stars were right and I flashed my roll discreetly, there'd be a willing cigarette girl to relieve my animal urges. All in all, it was an admirable establishment.

After leaving a couple of messages at the front desk of the Kipling I lost track of Lawe, but a few of his clothes remained in the dresser. Even if I had to pay it all myself, the rent was still cheap, so I stayed until the dog racing season came to a close at the end of July.

I was most often lucky at cards and dice, but I hit a bad stretch and funds began to run low. Even though I was young and had my health, I decided to seek employment. By now I had seen many of the fillum stars in person at the clubs. As a lot, they were smaller than I had imagined. When I saw them on the silver screen they were always bigger than life. In the club they were rather ignorable. I felt that perhaps I, too, was meant to be a movie star.

I had made some impression on the movie crowd with my dancing and had plied many of them with liquor. I let it be known that I was looking for work in fillum. Sadly, Joseph Kennedy had already left Hollywood, leaving his studio in Howard Hughes' hands. Had he still been there, our mutual acquaintances from the liquor industry could have secured me a job at once and kept Capone off at the same time.

Still and all, there were enough Irish among the employees at Warner Brothers that a friend of a friend got me an audition.

Now there was a rude awakening. The casting director was a short little fairy by the name of Ralph. He had a puny mustache and a holier-than-thou attitude to go with it. He told me I was too tall, too bony, too red-headed to be a star.

"Fillums are black and white," said I. "How can the color of my hair have any bearing?"

"Where have you been?' said Ralph. "Every movie has to be 100% talking, 100% singing, 100% dancing, and 100% color."

"Since when?"

"Since 1929."

We went back and forth for a while because I said I hadn't seen many color motion pictures, and he said I should take a trip to the Technicolor lab, and it all got a little heated. To ease things, I took out a flask of the good stuff and offered him a snort. He fetched two of those folded paper cups from the Sparkletts cooler, and I poured the libations.

In the end—by which I mean four shots later—he allowed as how I was a serviceable dancer and found me some extra work. I think he was enamored of me, but I wasn't going down that tunnel.

~~~

I WORKED TWO silent walk-ons, as we actors call them: Man at Bar and Plug-Ugly #2. I had no lines but the acting was simple enough. I tried to make myself noticed, but

I was lost amidst so many hams. The one time I did get the director's attention he said to his assistant:

"Get that tall ugly feller to stop making faces at the camera."

I was shamed, and so I moved myself to the background. Here I heard the seeds of discontent being sown by those extras who never got to be close to the camera or have their faces featured.

How my heart was gladdened to hear that the socialists and communists had come to help organize the workers in Tinseltown. The German, Italian, and Spanish fascists had driven them out of their own lands and they flocked to Hollywood. I could see that given time the Confederation of Studio Unions would grow into a force to be reckoned with. I spent many an hour in economic debate about the evils of capitalism and the coming revolution there amongst the backdrops of the movie sets.

Warner Brothers had made two brilliant gangster films, *Little Caesar* with Edgar G. Robinson and *Public Enemy* with James Cagney. This gave rise to much discussion among the socialist faction.

One particularly angry woman in her fifties claimed to be Emma Goldman, but I thought that unlikely. She had a compelling manner, to be sure.

"The popularity of gangster movies signals the end of capitalism," said Emma. "We make heroes of thieves and murderers because that is all that is left to the working man if he wants to survive this economic collapse."

Another fellow, an extra often cast because of his long jowls and hangdog expression added, "All property is theft, sister."

"And you cannot truly steal what is already stolen, comrade," said Emma.

I wasn't so sure about that and I noticed that the communists collected their wages as quick as the next fellow. And they didn't care to buy a round of drinks as any son of Erin would do. I left them to their own devices and gave thought to how to advance my career.

It was obvious, at least to me, that I knew the gangster world, and so I put it about the studio that I would be willing to serve as a technical advisor. Perhaps then my true worth would be recognized and I might rise to prominence in filmdom.

Nothing came of that, though. Even so I was paying my rent and working in fillum.

I myself was a big fan of the all singing all dancing musicals of the past couple of years, like *King of Jazz* and *Kiss Me Again*. So you can imagine my delight when I heard that Warner Brothers was undertaking a gangster musical to be called *Tommy Gun Tim*, about a rum runner whose weapon of choice was a Thompson submachine gun. His life becomes complicated when he falls in love with a beautiful taxi dancer who is fond of the tango. The rumor was they were hoping to double their audience by offering the singing and dancing for the ladies, while the tough guys and gunplay would satisfy the menfolk.

I went at once to Ralph the casting director and gave him the glad eye, raising his hopes.

"Say, I heard *Tommy Gun Tim* needs dancers," said I.

He looked at me coyly. "But these dancers also have to be able to play tough."

I grabbed Ralph by the lapels of his coat, lifting him until he was on tiptoe and pulled him close enough that he felt my breath on his cheek. I snarled into his startled face, which had gone pale.

"Like this, aye? Tough enough for ye?" I set him down again.

He blinked rapidly and blushed with desire.

"Oh my," said Ralph. "I'm sure I can find something."

~~~

ONCE THE WARDROBE department was finished with me I was a glorious sight, what with the top hat and swallowtails, spats and gloves. They even issued me a superb full-bark Malacca walking stick.

A dancing master wearing a bow tie surveyed the lines of men and women ready for the number. He paired me with a gorgeous article, a petite blond featherweight who someday would feed her babbies well. The outfit they had poured her into left little to the imagination, though I must say mine began working overtime.

And she had the tiniest feet, strapped into white satin shoes with five-inch heels. I realized that without the shoes she must be no more than five feet tall.

She gave me a look, such as might have come from a much older woman. Sizing me up from soles to crown.

"You're a long drink of water," she said.

I stepped closer and swept off my topper, bowing.

"Aloysius Haine, at your service." Trying for the grand impression, don't you know.

She tried to hide a smile.

"So. You're a redhead, too."

"Guilty as charged, Miss—?"

"Barton-Poole."

"Miss Barton-Poole."

"Is it true what they say about redheads?"

I had heard so many things I hardly knew where to

start. "That Judas was a redhead? That red hair means a fiery temper? That you should spit over your shoulder and ward off the evil eye when you meet one?"

She shook her head no, making the little spit curl next her ear bounce oh, so becomingly.

"The way I heard it was 'Red on top, fire below.'"

I am not sure, but I think I fell in love at that moment. Or at least lust.

"You think like a man," I said.

"Brother, you don't know the half of it."

I was tempted to put her over my shoulder and head for the nearest motel. Instead we repaired to our respective dressing areas and changed into rehearsal clothes.

~~~

"Children! Children!" called a fey voice. I turned to see the dancing master waving us all into place. "My name is Mercutio. I shall be your dance instructor. We are going to work on the cli-*mac*-tic number of the movie, a large scale divertissement called the 'Tommy Gun Tango'."

"Cli-*mac*-tic?" said Gayle sotto voce. "I bet he can hardly contain himself."

I snorted as I tried to choke off my laughter, drawing a withering glance from Mercutio. I gave him back my most dazzling smile.

"Let us focus our attention, children," said he. "Follow my lead. And a one, two, three, four..."

We began the rehearsal process which went on for nearly three hours before we broke for lunch. Ralph dropped by the commissary and stopped at the table where Gayle and I were mangling some rubbery lamb chops. He said he just wanted to "make

BRANT RANDALL AND BRUCE COOK

sure I had found the rehearsal studio all right."

After he left I realized that Gayle had stopped eating and was looking at me in wonder.

"I thought I could always tell," said Gayle. "You sure fooled me."

"And how would I have done that?" I said.

She gave me a limp-wristed wave and said, "Oh, you know."

I stared at her as she forked another bite of lamb into the abyss.

"I guess I should have known, you being so interested in dance," she said. "But…"

I pushed back from the table and offered her my hand.

"It's time to get back to rehearsal," I said. "However, I would like to take you to dinner tonight and see if I can demonstrate my true nature."

I wasn't sure, but I thought she might have smiled a wee bit as we left the dining room.

~~~

LATER THAT NIGHT, after a most satisfactory demonstration, we lay side by side on the Murphy bed in her modest apartment. I was covered in sweat, having put in extra effort to make sure she was completely sated. I had nearly fallen asleep when she rose from the tangled sheets and padded barefoot to the kitchenette, as naked and shameless as the day she was born.

I heard the tinkle of ice in a glass, and she came back with gin on the rocks. She stood beside the bed, her body gleaming white in the shaft of moonlight that slanted through the window, and threw back a long gulp before handing me the glass.

It was a wonder to watch the play of muscle and flesh as she stretched her arm toward me, her breast just grazing my wrist. It almost made me believe in God again.

I took the beaker, pushing myself upright against the headboard. I saluted her, swallowed a draught, and said, "And here's to colleens, may all the saints bless them."

She climbed into bed and sat cross-legged before me, searching my soul with her intense gaze. At last she came to a decision.

"I think we can do some business together," Miss Barton-Poole said. "There'll be enough money for the both of us."

I felt a little shiver of anticipation in my gut—though it may have been only a resurgence of lust, seeing her silvery nude body displayed like that.

I've heard those words and that tone of voice before. It was the voice of someone with a con game to run. And I was ready to listen. No doubt about it.

I was in love.

MISS ILONA'S
HOLLYWOOD SCRAPBOOK
PART III: *MABEL NORMAND*

HOLLYWOOD'S DAILY TATTLER

MABEL NORMAND: TINSELTOWN'S FADING STAR!

--February 25, 1922

Though Mabel Normand was questioned by police, she was never considered a serious suspect in the shooting of William Desmond Taylor. But her friendship with Taylor—which she always claimed was nothing more than platonic, even though love letters from her were found in Taylor's apartment—has further tarnished her reputation. Police investigators have also uncovered that Miss Normand has a $2,000 per month cocaine habit.

That's right! Two thousand dollars per month for that pernicious substance! And that at a time when many an American family lives on less than that amount for an entire year. What excess! What sin! What decadence! Hollywood should no longer be known as Tinseltown, but rather its new name should be Sodom by the Sea!

And as the guilty so often do, Miss Normand (former paramour of Mack Sennett, close friend of the disgraced Fatty Arbuckle, last person known to have seen William Desmond Taylor alive) has decided to get out of town until things settle down. We hear she is planning an extended trip to Europe.

Currently her films are banned in several cities, both here and abroad.

MABEL NORMAND: FALLING STAR!
--January 2, 1924

Mabel Normand is in the news again. It wasn't so long ago that her pal Fatty Arbuckle was accused of murder. And then a few months later her lover William Desmond Taylor was murdered. Of course she was never formally accused of anything in either case.

It seems Mabel's chauffeur is accused of the attempted murder of oil driller Courtland Dines. The shooting took place at a New Year's party Mr. Dines was throwing at his apartment, which Miss Normand attended. Interestingly, Edna Perviance (Chaplin's former leading lady, both on screen and off) was also present. Rumor has it that she is engaged to Mr. Dines.

The police have in custody one Joe Kelly, Miss Normand's driver.

MORE ON MABEL!

--January 10, 1924

The police investigation of the shooting of Courtland S. Dines, oil tycoon, has turned up bizarre evidence against the accused shooter, Joe Kelly. It seems that isn't his real name. He was known as Horace Greer when he escaped from a San Francisco chain gang! He has been living in Los Angeles and working under an assumed name for some time now...

And once again Mabel has *not* been named as a suspect in the attempted murder of Courtland S. Dines on New Year's Eve—even though the police know the pistol involved in the shooting belongs to her!

The police have Horace Greer, Miss Normand's chauffeur, in custody.

MORE ON MABEL'S CHAUFFEUR: HE DIDN'T DO IT! SO WHO DONE IT?

--June 20, 1924

Horace Greer, ex-chauffeur for Mabel Normand, film actress, late Thursday was acquitted by a jury in superior court on charges of assault to commit murder on

Courtland S. Dines, a Denver, Colorado, oil operator.

Greer, who refused to testify in his own defense because, he said, he would "rather go to the penitentiary than say anything that would hurt Miss Normand" watched the jurors closely as Fricke was completing the arguments.

His decision to stay off the witness stand, which caused the attorneys to throw up their hands in consternation, was made at the last minute, after his attorneys had promised he would testify and "tell everything."

Prosecutors were stumped by the inability of any other witness to remember anything clearly. This may have been because, as Miss Normand stated, "They had all been drinking quite a bit."

Well pardon us! Isn't that a violation of the 18th Amendment of the Constitution?

Witnesses Mabel Normand and Edna Perviance agreed that Mr. Dines was in his undershirt in the bedroom with Miss Perviance, while Miss Normand powdered her nose nearby. They agreed that they heard a knock at the door and Mr. Dines went to answer it, and it was Normand's chauffeur who was at the door. They agreed that they heard a sound "like three firecrackers going off." And they agreed that they saw Dines covered in blood and that they helped him onto the bed, and then called for an ambulance.

Testimony reveals that the weapon used was Miss Normand's automatic .25 pistol. She "hadn't seen it in months and months," though "it used to reside in my nightstand."

The *Tattler* says *Really?*

Mr. Greer testified that a drunken Dines came after him with a whiskey bottle and that he shot the oilman in self defense.

Mr. Dines declined to testify against the man charged with his attempted murder. Was he afraid of what he might have to reveal under cross-examination?

Outside the courtroom Dines says that Greer was "full of hop."

So we have a shooting, consumption of illegal alcohol, drugs, and various unrelated parties in a state of undress—but the courts can find nothing wrong!

The *Tattler* wonders who got paid off.

Currently Normand's films are banned (again) in several cities, both here and abroad.

MABEL NORMAND: TINSELTOWN'S FALLING STAR!

--September 15, 1924

Mabel Normand was named yesterday in the divorce dispute of the very wealthy couple, Norman and Georgia Church. Mrs. Church, in the complaint against her husband, claimed Church had imparted to her that Mabel had amorous meetings with him while he was in the hospital in August of 1923.

At that time Mabel was in the hospital recovering from a broken collarbone received in a fall from a horse. Even though the complaint has been lodged by Mrs. Church against her husband, Miss Normand wants the opportunity to vindicate herself.

Yet again her films are banned in several cities, both here and abroad.

OH MABEL! HER TARNISHED STAR HAS SET!

--February 15, 1925

Norman Church has retracted what he had told his wife, concerning alleged amorous affairs between himself and Miss Normand. Mrs. Church for her part has apologized to Mabel.

Meanwhile, after several months of tawdry publicity, Mabel has lost her action in the suit on the grounds she did not have direct interest in the matter. The judge said that although her name was brought up, her guilt or innocence ultimately was not pertinent to the main issue.

Currently her films are banned—we think permanently this time—in several cities, both here and abroad.

Miss Normand says she is retiring to private life.

GAYLE BARTON-POOLE

When it is dark enough,
One can see the stars.
— *Persian Proverb*

one~
MGM Follies
May 1932

THERE WAS A knock on the dressing room door. From the other side I heard Sid, the second assistant director, call out:

"Miss Poole, are you ready? All the other talent is on set."

I looked into the mirror. The peroxide job was great, and my hair was an even ash blonde, just like Jean Harlow's. My eyebrows were penciled in with a Claudette Colbert arch. All in all, *I* was looking good.

But my costume, that was something else. I was supposed to be secretary to the big boss, and they put me in this Miss Mouse outfit that wasn't fit for anything but an old folks home.

I undid the top button of the blouse, but it didn't bring

my cleavage into view. I took a pair of bobby socks out of my purse and stuffed them into the underside of my brassiere.

That was the ticket. Nice fat, cream-white puppies struggled to get out of my blouse.

Sid pounded on my dressing room door. "Poole, if you don't get your can on set, they are going to recast the part."

"Hold your water," I said. "I'm coming."

I unlocked the door and swept past Sid. He skipped to catch up with me, and once he came abreast—if you catch my drift—he gargled for a couple of seconds and grabbed my arm.

"Gayle, I'm gonna tell you this as a friend. You can't go onto the set with your...your...I mean they're just hanging out like that. If the Hayes code guys catch sight of those, those—"

"Is bosoms the word you're searching for, Sid?" I said. "I believe most ladies have them. It's hard to understand what Mr. Hayes has against them. Some hormonal deficiency, no doubt."

He clutched my arm a little harder, hurting me. "But, but you're supposed to be a secretary to the president of a large corporation, not a common tramp."

"Let me go." I slapped his hand away. "You're bruising the merchandise." And I marched onto the set.

Things were busy, Hollywood busy. Half a dozen electricians and grips were making final adjustments to the lights and flags, adjusting a shadow line so it would fall across the boss' desk just at the right angle. The director of photography didn't think they were moving fast enough and told them so in language that turned the air blue.

The camera crew was switching out a film magazine

on the huge Mitchell camera. The first assistant cameraman got busy threading the film through the innards of the monster.

The director sat in his chair at one edge of the set talking with the film's lead, Edgar G. Robinson. A makeup artist powdered Robinson's forehead, getting rid of the sweat sheen that working under the lights had brought out.

The first assistant director spotted me and rushed over. He was a skinny little swish who got his job because he was the nephew of one of the studio owners. He gave me a look that could have pickled eggs.

"So glad you could make it, Miss Poole," he said with a sniff. "Fortunately for you the cameraman has been having a bit of drama with his crew or we would all be waiting on you. And Hollywood doesn't wait on bit players. It replaces them."

He peered at my chest with distaste, and motioned that I should follow him to speak with the director. It all went downhill from there.

The way Mr. Robinson licked the cigar he was puffing made it clear that he approved of my outfit, but the director had a conniption fit. He clutched his hair like some ham actor in a silent film and then waved his arms like he was doing semaphore. He was a recent immigrant, a "genius" from Europe, trying to make his mark in American film, and he was afraid I was going to queer his big break. When at last he found his voice, the accent was so thick I didn't know what he was jawing about.

So I just stood there and smiled at him. I've got a great dimple in my cheek—and a couple of others I show my friends. I've found the dimple is better at getting me what I want than most arguments I can think up.

I didn't understand his jabber but I'm guessing that he was another swish, because the dimple wasn't working. He didn't come off the boil. Instead, his face got red, his voice got louder, and he began to spray little drops of spit. To my surprise he reached over and tried to button my blouse, making plenty of contact with my breast while he did so.

I stiffened my spine, put on what they call a haughty look—you know, the kind Constance Bennett does so well—and slapped him square across the face. I saw the other crew people back away, though his assistant smiled behind the director's back, and I figured I was going to get canned. Still, the story would be sure to get around, and any publicity is good publicity.

But at that moment a little squirrel of a fellow—another European, by the look of him—came over and calmed Mister Big Shot Director down. It played out like a class reunion between fellow catamites. After a bit the squirrel took me by the elbow and walked me to the stage door.

"You couldn't understand a word he said, could you?"

"That wasn't the King's English, I should think," I said.

"I suppose he thought it was, though." He laughed and offered me his hand. "My name is Paul Bern."

He paused like he was waiting for me to recognize him and say something.

"I am so pleased to meet you, Mr. Bern. I am Gayle Barton-Poole," I said, and shook his hand with just the ends of my fingers, the way I had seen English women do.

"Would you care to have coffee with me, Miss Poole?"

"Sorry to be difficult, but it's Barton-Poole, with a

hyphen. The merging of two families back in Shropshire, don't you know."

"You're from England?" He gave a funny half smile and said, "Please forgive my mistake with your name. I still would like to offer you coffee."

~~~

WE WALKED PAST several sound stages, huge empty warehouses big enough to park the Graf Zeppelin dirigible, and made our way toward the studio commissary. The passageways between the stages were full of actors in makeup, technicians moving their gear, and studio messengers on their bicycles.

Once inside the commissary Bern was very polite, fetching coffee and pastries for me.

He also made sure our table was out of the way so we could talk privately.

He was very kind and sympathetic. He told me the director had someone more dowdy in mind to be the secretary.

"Have you ever seen any dowdy secretaries in large offices, Mr. Bern?" I said. "I haven't."

He grimaced. "Only when the boss' wife chooses them." He took another sip of coffee, which I could see was mostly milk and sugar. "The director didn't want someone so flashy in the office scene. He feared it would take attention away from the stars."

"Quite."

"And he also pointed out that you look a great deal like Jean Harlow."

"Oh, do you think so?" Secretly I was pleased by this news.

He blinked rapidly at that and went on. "The audience might think you really are Jean. It wouldn't do for the audiences to think that she was taking bit—er, smaller roles now that she has achieved star status."

"You think she and I look that much alike?"

"It's a remarkable resemblance."

"I don't see it. I'm much younger than she."

His eyes darted around in discomfort, and he ended by staring at my upper arm.

"You have some bruises on your bicep. It almost looks like fingers gripped you."

"A certain assistant director jerked me around on the way to the set." I fingered my arm and pretended it was tender. "Speaking of the set, I probably ought to get back."

He couldn't take his eyes away from the marks and licked his lips twice.

"I'm afraid you no longer have a role on that film." He looked up once again.

"That's hardly fair, is it? And I need the work. These are difficult times."

"I will try to get you other work."

"Perhaps I could work as a double for Miss Harlow."

His eyes became troubled. "I'm not sure about that." He glanced at his wristwatch. "I'm overdue for a meeting. Perhaps we can discuss this over dinner tonight."

"That would be ever so lovely."

"I'll make a reservation at the Cocoanut Grove. Can you meet me there at eight?" I nodded. "Ask for Maurice and you'll to be taken to my table."

He excused himself and hurried away. I spent another few minutes finishing my Danish and seeing who else was in the dining room. I liked looking for stars, seeing if I could catch them picking their teeth with their elbows on the table.

It had taken me six weeks to engineer this meeting with Bern, but I had the feeling we were going to be great friends.

I might even show him my dimples.

two~
How I Got to Hollywood
November 1929

IT WAS THREE years since I left home. Peony Springs is a little dump of a town in that part of the Appalachians that runs through western Massachusetts. Didn't have a roller rink or a movie theater. If it hadn't been for my grampa and gramma taking me and my brothers to the next town every month or, so I never would have seen a movie. That's how I found my calling.

I'm meant to be a movie star. I've got the face and I've got the body and boy, can I act. I don't make faces the way half those hams on the silver screen do. Like Joan Crawford. Or Clara Bow, that "it" girl.

And I have more "it" than Bow ever thought about.

Or as Dorothy Parker said, "*It!* Hell, she has *those.*" Bow may have "those" but mine are better.

Truth to tell, I once spent an afternoon on a movie set with Clara. I was new to Hollywood back in '29, just after the stock market crash. I had myself a job as an extra in a film called *The Wild Party* and danced the black bottom in the background.

While the set was being redressed for the next scene—which meant spreading a lot of trash and broken lamps around to show the party was over—Clara went off to one side to have a toot, but her bottle was empty. She cursed up a storm, and I learned a few words new to me. She was positive somebody had been drinking up her private stock.

It so happened that I always carried my own supply wherever I went in Hollywood, it being Prohibition and all. The mayor of Los Angeles was a Dry, a peckerhead who didn't think anyone else ought to enjoy themselves either, so booze wasn't out in the open like some other places.

Anyhow, I went over to Clara and hiked up the hem of my flapper dress, letting her see the flask I had tucked in the top of my stocking. She gave me kind of a funny look, and later on I heard she sometimes did three ways, so maybe she thought I was coming on to her.

I pulled out the flask and shook it so she could hear it gurgle. Quick as dammit she grabbed it, unscrewed the cap, and took a swallow.

My, oh my! That gal could put it away. Still, I don't think she'd ever run up against anything as hot as DeCosta's Special Blend of corn likker and grappa. The tip of her nose went red and her eyes watered while she struggled to get her breath back.

"Oh, baby. That's raw," she said. "Raw, but good."

After that she and I became like sisters. At least until we finished the flask.

The set dressers were taking their sweet time, so I undid my Symington side lacer, let the girls have a little breathing space. I saw Clara take a sideways look and shake her head.

"Who had the lame idea women oughta look like boys? We got too many fairies designing outfits for us gals. And I ain't met a real man who didn't like a full hand. Get their faces in between and just dream of mama."

That got us laughing pretty hard and called for another drink or three.

She told me a few stories about how she got started back in silent films, and how she had played it fast and loose. The way she talked, it was obvious she was the most common kind of woman, from a trashy background.

"So how'd you get your big break?" I said, after she had downed half a dozen shots.

"Ain't no secret how to make your way in Hollywood," she said. "It's who you know and who you blow."

When you put it that way, I guess it isn't that much of a secret.

~~~

I HAD LEFT Peony Springs and made it to Hollywood three years ago. I had written my parents a couple of times but they hadn't responded, so guess I was as dead to them as they were to me.

When I got here I had just passed my fourteenth birthday. Of course my physical endowments made people think I was older. I told everyone I was seventeen, not wanting to disappoint folks. And saying I was still under age kept me out of certain problems.

On one occasion I thought they were going to catch on to my real age. I was working on a racy film over at Universal Studios, and they asked to see a proof of birth. It seems someone had employed a sixteen-year-old in a risqué scene and when the girl's father saw the movie and recognized his little princess, he complained to the police. It was only after multiple payoffs that the studio had avoided being charged with a violation of the Mann Act.

At the time I had been out of work for a month, so I really needed a job. I struck on a brilliant notion. I told them that the county courthouse where vital records were kept had burned down two years before, and I didn't see how I could produce a birth certificate.

The secretary I was talking to gave me the same kind of look my teacher did when I told her the dog ate my homework. She told me this had come up before and they were willing to accept a baptismal record.

I asked around and I found an artful engraver in his late seventies who had a small shop near Westlake Park. For ten dollars Mr. Finkel would supply me with a suitably aged document.

He was an elderly man from Vienna who had shrunk to such a degree that he only came up to my chin. I could count on one hand the white hairs that he combed over his liver-spotted scalp. He showed me an example of a birth certificate of somebody named Ludwig van Beethoven, handwritten on parchment. It looked a thousand years old.

"And I made this just yester*tag*," he said with a proud smile. "It's a birthday present for a musician *freund* of mine."

This was interesting in its own right and opened up several possibilities for me. I had on a blouse of severe décolletage. I asked him how he did such marvelous work, leaning forward over the counter of his storefront shop so he could get an eyeful. He drank in the view and invited me back into his workroom.

"Listen, Mr. Finkel, I wasn't born yesterday," I said, giving him coy smile number three. "Aren't you supposed to offer me candy if you want to lure me into some dark room?"

The old man pursed his lips in disapproval. With the stray whiskers he had missed shaving that morning his mouth looked like the puckered rear end of a short haired terrier.

"Please, Miss Palmer. Such things I am beyond. But if you want to see how this is done you must into my workshop come."

I figured I could knock him over with one hand tied behind me, as old and shriveled as he was, so I followed him behind the counter. He showed me a whole selection of papers, of differing rag and fiber content; he showed me a small hand-cranked press where he set the type himself; he showed me fountain pens and quills, bottles of ink made from an enormous variety of pigments; and he showed me his ovens.

"What do you need ovens for?"

His eyes twinkled. "But this is how we age the document. A few days at a hundred degrees centigrade, a light wash of Ceylon tea, some hours of exposure to this ultraviolet lamp and we have a beautiful old document— made this week."

~~~

IT SO HAPPENED that although Mr. Finkel was beyond some things, he still liked to look. I gave him a little free show, with him licking his whiskery wrinkled lips over and over. It ended with him giving me the baptismal certificate, no charge at all. Satisfaction on both sides.

I foresaw that I would be doing other business with Mr. Finkel whenever I saw the use for a new identity. I just hoped he wouldn't croak until after I needed him.

three~
Broadway and the Broad Way
February 1930

YOU MAY HAVE noticed that Mr. Finkel called me
Miss Palmer. That's because my real name is Jackie Sue
Palmer. I'm not English and I don't know Shropshire from
sheepdip. I floundered for a while before I came up with
the British actress wheeze.

It didn't take long living in LA to find out Hollywood
wasn't even a real city, just kind of a neighborhood
where the trolley line passes. I first took a room at the
YWCA and eventually moved into a studio apartment on
Beachwood just north of Franklin, right down the hill from the
Hollywoodland sign. Most of my early film work was
doing background work—as they called the extra
players—in westerns. There were a passel of low-budget
companies on Gower, so many that they called the area
Gower Gulch.

There was a breakfast spot at the Hollywood
Boulevard corner of Gower called the Copper Skillet
where all the movie cowboys got their morning feed. I

discovered that if I made friends with them, I worked more regular. Plus they were easy to be friendly with. When they found out I could milk a cow, they knew I was a country gal.

I got a few bit parts here and there: a bargirl in a saloon, an Indian maiden who gets shot, a waitress. Kept thinking I'd be discovered. Mostly I was hoping I could use those credits in westerns to get some work at Paramount or RKO, which were only a couple of blocks further south. Those studios paid better and their movies got seen by bigger audiences. They also had better-known stars.

I began using the Red Cars to travel down south to MGM in Culver City, up north to Warner Brothers in Burbank, or further west to Fox.

Did I say LA was spread out? I met plenty of gals from New York who were just plain appalled that the place was so huge.

I was talking to a background dancer named Jacqueline Houchin, used to be a Rockette, had legs up to here. She always wore her dresses an inch or two higher above the knee than anyone else. Spent good money on her clothes, but made up for it by not owning any underwear. She'd heard how Ruby Keeler had used her gams to snare a bunch of Broadway roles and ended up married to Al Jolson, so Jacqueline had come to Hollywood. I told her I thought Ruby had used more than her gams.

Anyway.

"Whose crazy idea was it to make this city so big and rambling?" she said. "New York's got a lot bigger population than Los Angeles and you don't see us spreading all over the state."

"No one made you come here, Jacqueline."

"And there's no real downtown, no center where all the action is," she said. "I mean, what's the pernt?"

"I'm not sure the planners down at city hall think there has to be a point," I said.

"City hall? Don't get me started," she said. "They call that runt of a building a skyscraper. In New York it would be Chrysler's little brother."

"Personally, I like being able to see the sky out here."

"Why do you need to see so much of it? I can see all I want in Central Park. And you have to take a streetcar ten miles to get from one good store to the next. In New York there's a great store on the next block."

To tease her I began calling ten miles an LA block and advising the Manhattan girls they should probably move back to NYC before their little legs wore down to nubs.

I didn't need any more competition. Gorgeous girls from all over the planet kept arriving in Hollywood, hoping that their face would make their fortune. They were pitiful, as dumb as bricks. At first they'd be all uppity about how they were saving themselves for their boyfriends back home, and after they'd become a star they'd go back and have that family they really wanted. In a few months it was all about how they'd save themselves for the right man, someone who'd see them for the precious jewel they really were.

Then it was the right producer. Or director. Or casting director. Or cameraman. Or agent.

Or anyone with five bucks. Maybe less.

Lot of those gals wore out more than one mattress before they took their sorry goods back to Kansas or Budapest or wherever the hell they came from.

I think it might have been simpler back when Clara Bow got her start. The men who worked in Hollywood nowadays thought they was living in a candy store and everything was free.

~~~

I WAS LUNCHING in the Paramount commissary, waiting to be discovered as I picked at my piece of apple pie with a slice of cheddar. In the booth behind me some English gent sat down with a little guy who had a heavy New York accent. I listened in like I always do, because you pick up interesting business tips that way. Or sometimes a bit of gossip you can put to good use later on.

They were talking about how the movies were going to go one hundred percent musical and trying to put some deal together. The English geezer went by the name of Woodlouse if I heard right—and from the other Brits I had met I knew any name was possible, no matter how crazy it sounded. Anyway, he was planning the best way to approach some producer.

"Jerry, I'm certain we can get them to make a film of our stage play *Sitting Pretty.*"

I snickered at that. Back in Peony Springs "sitting pretty" meant a gal had the crotch of her panties visible to those seated across the room.

"Why would they want to film that old warhorse?" said the New Yorker. "We sent the road company out to the sticks three years ago. The audience is used up for that one."

"One of the producers here on the lot is an orphan, and the orphans in the story will appeal to him. It's a question of discerning the psychology of the individual and then shaping our pitch to take advantage." He

went on for another five minutes but I had stopped
listening.

That passing remark struck a chord in me. I realized
I had to improve my strategy if I was going to get the
career that was rightfully mine.

I left a tip by my pie plate and walked back up Gower
to Hollywood Boulevard, then headed east looking for a
place I had seen in my daily walks.

~~~

I FOUND THE bookstore I had remembered, went
inside, and struck up a conversation with the salesclerk,
a tall, toothy girl with a huge chest and saucer-like blue
eyes. She was so dim she thought she'd be discovered
working in a print emporium. She did seem to enjoy her
chewing gum, though. She told me her name was Linda
and wondered if she could help me.

"I find that I need to bone up on psychology," I said.
"Can you recommend something?"

She stared at me for about three seconds while her
brain processed my request. "I think I heard of that," she
said and walked lackadaisically into an alcove stuffed
with books in dark bindings.

She came back with a couple of volumes. She handed
me the first, *Three Essays on the Theory of Sexuality*, by
someone named Sigmund Freud. It was bound in quality
linen with the title stamped in gold.

"This is the one most males are interested in," she said,
putting a particular emphasis on the word males.

I cracked it open and read a couple of paragraphs in
the middle of the book. Pure gibberish as far as I could
make out.

"Is this supposed to be in English?" I said. I read aloud

from the book. "We found it a regrettable thing that the existence of the sexual instinct in children has been denied and that the sexual manifestations not infrequently to be observed in children have been described as irregularities. It seemed to us on the contrary that children bring germs of sexual activity with them into the world, that they already enjoy sexual satisfaction when they begin to take nourishment and that they persistently seek to repeat the experience in the familiar activity of 'thumb sucking.'"

I snapped the book shut and looked at Blue Eyes.

She stared back, chewing with some concentration.

"Germs of sexual activity?" I said. "Thumb sucking brings sexual satisfaction?"

"Most people find Frood to be pretty raw when they read it straight from the horse's mouth. So I usually sell them this one the next day."

She handed me a much thinner book printed on cheap paper with a cardboard cover.

"*Frood for Everyman,*" I said, reading the title. "That sounds more like it." I flipped through it, discovering that were several interesting pictures illustrating dreams. Also the type was larger and there were headlines here and there, like *Oral Fixations* and *Deviance.* "I'll take it."

She stood there for a few moments and then said. "That will be a dollar ninety-five." She popped her gum. "Cash."

And I'd been hoping to trade her a dozen eggs.

~~~

I WON'T SAY Freud was easy going, but I did begin to see new possibilities in the way I dealt with people. And by people I meant men. Women I just ignored or moved out of my way.

Plus his ideas about interpreting dreams led me to start keeping a diary of my own. I wasn't sure why I was doing so, but I figured there might be something of value in those dreams. If nothing else, I could turn them into good pillow talk.

I tried sucking my thumb a few times but couldn't seem to get it working.

four~
Going to Temple
Summer 1931

WHERE I GREW up in Massachusetts, Jews was about as scarce as Chinese, meaning I hadn't ever met any. But once I started in the film biz, I met more than I could count.

I wondered aloud about it one day when I was doing extra work at Columbia. I was standing by the unfinished backside of a ballroom set, waiting for my entrance cue. Sam Duncan, the foreman of the studio carpenters at Columbia, was there making a repair to the door frame, and he told me his crackpot idea.

"You ever notice that the brass at every studio is a Jew?" Sam said. "It's a worldwide plot."

"A plot?" I said.

"Karl Marx and Vladimir Lenin were Jews, too."

"What do Marx and Lenin have to do with movies?"

"Communism will be spread by means of the cinema," said Sam. "It's explained in that book by Eisenstein."

"Who's Eisenstiny?"

"Another Commie Jew, and he just happens to be the top dog in Russian movies." He almost spit this last bit out, like it proved his point.

I guess I must have looked skeptical so he went on.

"The banks are all owned by Jews, too," he said. "Another part of the master plan."

"It's hard to see how banking and Communism are related," I said. "I mean aren't bankers capitalists, sort of on the other side from the communists?"

"Both sides are full of Jews."

He wasn't the only one to spout off about the "plot." From the blue collar workers behind the sets I heard even more rumors of various conspiracies and how the Jews wanted to take over the world through movie screens, though just how that would be accomplished was murky. Most of these deep thinkers thought the Depression was the first step toward something, even if they weren't sure what.

Could be the Apocalypse.

~~~

THE REASON THERE were so many Jews in Hollywood was pretty simple. All the studios but Disney had been started by some East European immigrant Jew or another. Every one of these guys had come from New York, and they all knew each other. Since the studios were family businesses, they hired brothers and nephews and in-laws and stole employees from each other till the whole industry was one incestuous mess of nepotism.

The only conspiracy they were involved in was who was going to make the most money. It was more like a contest to see who could be the biggest donor to this or that temple, temple being the Jew name for church. I remembered that fact from my Sunday School classes back in Peony Springs. From what I gathered, the studio big shots thought it would get them a place in Heaven living next door to Abraham and Moses. Maybe Jesus, too.

I spied Louis Mayer as he drove into MGM one morning. He had a limousine and a chauffeur and you would have thought he was president or the king of some small country the way people bowed and scraped as he went through the gates.

I didn't think my chance of meeting him on the lot was all that good, but I recalled that in my home town the bank president went to the same Methodist church as my dad and a lot of the farmers.

I decided I should start going to temple. Even if I didn't sit in the same pew as Mr. Mayer, maybe I could squeeze in next to his son-in-law or some other studio bigwig. I didn't know which temple was the right one, so I picked the one closest to where I lived.

~~~

ANGELUS TEMPLE WAS just a short ride by Red Car, so I went there one Saturday night. I knew that the Jews didn't worship on Sunday, though I wasn't clear why. Maybe it was something to do with them feeling bad about the Crucifixion, though to my mind it was the Romans—who were Italian, I think—that actually did the dirty work.

When I got off the streetcar near Echo Lake I thought there must be a carnival in town. Arc lights swept the sky and I could hear a band in the distance. Crowds of people in their Sabbath best walked north along the lakeshore.

There was a woman and her two school-age children walking my way so I joined with them. She gave me a smile so I said, "Is there something special going on at the lake tonight? I mean all the music and lights."

"Not at all," she said. "This is just a regular service at the temple."

"Looks like quite a crowd to me."

"This must be your first time."

Her kids gave her a look like they all shared some secret that I wasn't in on. I began to wonder what I was getting into.

A huge structure came into view. It had a massive dome and tower and twin radio masts on top emblazoned with the letters KFSG. There were more entry doors and Greek columns than I had ever seen on one building. Well, I *think* the columns were Greek; they might have been Roman or Babylonian. The point is that it was an impressive sight, and I figured the Jews were onto something big if they needed a place this size for them to worship in.

There was quite a crowd trying to get in, and I lost track of the lady and her kids. I squashed in with another group and worked my way inside. It was just as impressive inside as out.

I took a seat near the back. Not the very last row, but near enough the exit that I could quickly sally forth if things were just too boring. An organist was playing and I didn't recognize any of the tunes, so I guessed the Jews must have their own hymns and whatnot. The folks in my pew gave me a nod of greeting and I felt pretty much at home. Here I'd been expecting something exotic.

The man next to me whispered, "Welcome, sister."

"Thanks."

"This must your first time."

That unsettled me a mite. "Now how'd you know that?"

"Newcomers always look about, make sure there's a door close by before they take a seat." He chuckled and handed me a hymnal.

Of course I was just a rube from farm country, so I had to listen to the service awhile before I realized they weren't speaking Hebrew most of the time. It turned out this wasn't a Jewish temple at all. It was some new religion I hadn't heard of before, Four Square Gospel.

The headliner was a handsome woman in her thirties. Aimee Semple McPherson was a powerful preacher, and boy, did she know how to stage a great spectacle. She could have taught Cecile B. DeMille a thing or three. There were choirs—not just one, but two, and there was a full orchestra. There were men and women in costume acting out the story of Noah's Ark. Before I knew what was happening. there were animals parading down the aisle right next to me, two by two.

Now when you have an auditorium filled with five thousand people and you try to drag two sheep and two goats and two donkeys and two of I-don't-know-what-all through them, things are bound to get a little cockeyed.

An old woman, must have been in her fifties, sitting in front of me craned her neck to stare at the animals traipsing by. One of the donkeys rolled a jaundiced eye, then jerked its head to look her square in the face and brayed with a sound like the last trump.

The lady shrieked right back, "Glory!"

That made the donkey start bucking and kicking. The donkey's handler, a hefty young Mexican gal, had to jerk hard on the bridle and use all her weight to keep the animal from breaking loose and running wild through the crowd. The donkey bawled, the lady bellowed, and then the donkey snapped its huge yellow teeth at her, almost catching her nose.

She—the lady, I mean—fainted dead away. Fell face down over the pew ahead of her, her flower print dress hiked up, showing her bloomers to the crowd. I thought it would cause a scandal, but people around me hardly turned a hair. An elderly man next to her just reached over and tugged her dress into place and carried on like nothing special had happened.

What with the animals—which, by the way, did not make me pine for the family farm—and folks fainting and Aimee hollering over the microphone system and the orchestra and the choirs singing back and forth at each other like it was a contest, it was some time before I was able to focus my attention again.

As I said, I went to Sunday school as a girl, so I was somewhat familiar with the story of Noah. I thought Aimee put a peculiar twist on it.

"And so God could only find the family of Noah that was righteous. He got them on that ark and then He sent a Great Flood." She paused here and beamed a thousand-watt smile over the multitude. "A Great Flood that covered the whole earth."

She went so far as likening the Great Flood to the Great Depression, in what my 8th grade English teacher would have called a strained comparison.

The audience went for it big, though, and began shouting *Amen!* and *Hallelujah!* and *Preach it, Sister Aimee!*

And Aimee did. She talked about sin, and she cried about salvation, and she argued about the state of damnation the United States was facing. She got to campaign shouting like a Southern Democrat. By the time she talked about God wiping the wicked from the face of the earth, she had worked the audience up to fever pitch. All at once Aimee stopped sermonizing and looked out over the crowd.

I did, too, and saw that there were a fair number of Negroes, Orientals, Mexicans, and maybe some Gypsies mixed among them. And every one of them, regardless of color, waited with bated breath to hear what came next.

Aimee leaned right up close to the microphone and stage whispered, "Let's take it to the Lord in prayer."

She raised her hands towards Heaven and began to speak aloud, her eyes closed, her body swaying. I couldn't make out what she was saying. It sounded like a foreign language, and I later learned that this was what they called speaking in tongues.

Not to be outdone, most of the congregation raised their own hands, closed their eyes, swayed back and forth, and began to gabble. Not quietly to themselves, but at full volume, like they thought God might be hard of hearing.

If you stand in the midst of five thousand people who are carrying on like that, all I can say is it's electrifying. I kind of froze in place and looked around in amazement, wondering how long this could go on, but kind of glad that they had forgotten to take the offering. Though to be fair, I would have put something in the basket, as I hadn't been so entertained in a good while.

Just then the lady who had fainted came back to life. She stood bolt upright, craned her neck back. Her eyes rolled up in their sockets and she began to yodel. She ululated—I believe that is the technical term—in a register even the pipe organ couldn't match. The dogs up on Noah's Ark began to howl in response.

The hairs on my arms and the back of my neck stood to attention, and I clutched my pocketbook pretty tight. The yodeler began to gyrate in place, her arms flung wide. Her neighbors in the pew moved out of the way, not wanting black eyes. She spun out into the aisle and began a jerking, spinning kind of dance that took her three steps forward, two steps back, one to the left, one to the right, but always led her toward the stage.

As soon as she began to move well, a dozen others joined her, arms raised, heads back, praying at the top of their lungs. In a couple of minutes there were hundreds in the aisles, snake-dancing their way down to get close to Sister Aimee.

For her part, Sister Aimee seemed unaware of the ruckus. Or else it was so common as not to need her attention.

~~~

AS THE COMMOTION became general I took the opportunity to slip out one of the many doors and head back to my apartment. At the streetcar stop I found a woman holding a cigarette in her hands, rummaging in her purse for a match. She was a looker, but wasn't wearing any makeup and had on the kind of shapeless dress I wouldn't be caught dead in. I stopped to give her a light and lit up a Philip Morris of my own.

"Thanks," she said. "You done already?"

"Done with what?"

She looked me up and down, exhaled a plume of smoke through her nose. "Go on. I can spot an actress at twenty paces."

"Sure I work in movies, but so? Done with what?" I said.

"I couldn't finish tonight. Migraine, you know. That speaking in tongues would've taken off the top of my head."

I thought it over and figured the angle. "So they put a few ringers in the crowd? Why?"

"Make sure things get off to a solid start. After a bit the true believers carry the ball. But the church elders don't like leaving things to chance."

It made sense. Dollars and sense. I hadn't waited for the collection plate to pass, but Angelus Temple hadn't been paid for with pin money. "How much?"

"Five a service," she said.

"I guess that'd keep you in cigarettes."

She gave me a sideways glance. "There's service seven nights a week. Three times on Sunday."

I guess my mouth must have dropped open.

"If you like I'll introduce you, get you a regular gig." She gave a tight smile. "They prefer pretty girls, but you have to scrape off the lipstick and rouge, anything that makes you look too trampy."

I made sure I had her phone number before I got off at my stop.

~~~

A LOT OF different thoughts raced around my brain as I undressed for bed. I felt the need to tell someone about this experience. Maybe Jacqueline.

Something told me they didn't have this in New York, and that might make Jacqueline jealous. Put her in her place and get her to shut up about the joys of New Amsterdam.

But mostly, I thought about how I could turn this to my advantage.

I'm always thinking and planning. A girl has to look out for herself.

I haven't met the man yet who was worth sticking with.

five~
Dyed in the Wool
New Years 1932 and on

MY CAREER WAS stuck in a pothole. I picked up background work at the studios at least twice a month, and a bit part once a month. Plus I was a ringer at Angelus Temple pretty often, so I was paying bills, putting groceries on the table, and keeping up my manicure. All this without having to sleep around.

Except when I wanted to. And I wanted to pretty often, if for no other reason than to keep the ennui at bay.

As you can tell, I had improved my vocabulary. I did that by hanging out with writers. They always threw unusual words into their conversation, hoping to trip each other up. I knew how to play that one.

"I'm sorry, Dash (or William or Ernest or whatever). I don't know that word." I'd give them the wide-eyed, adoring look number two, like I was enthralled just to be in the presence of such a powerful intellect. "Please explain it to me."

And then he'd gas on for a couple of minutes. They

always thought it adorable that such a sweet young thing was interested in self improvement. This was usually accompanied by another round of drinks—those writers could really suck it down—and a squeeze of my thigh, hidden from view by the tablecloth in whatever restaurant or night club he'd taken me to.

You know, "someplace quiet, where we can talk." Apparently writers think that talk and grope are synonyms.

They were *so* transparent. I discovered that the main difference between men and boys was the amount of hair on their bodies. Sort of like it slipped off their head and crept downhill.

Me being a rural girl and all, they thought it was a rare treat to get some of my country possum. I had to laugh—but not out loud.

There were a number of them that offered to set me up in a little apartment of my own, somewhere near the studio, but I didn't care to be kept by any one guy. Besides, it meant I'd lose my studio contacts with the others.

I also went out with a couple of handsome actors, but found them to be inferior in most respects. They were too used to women falling all over them. And they always wanted to go to well-lit nightclubs where there was a chance some newsman would spot us, snap a picture, and write a gossip item. Well, I am always in favor of publicity, but these big lugs always tried to crowd me out of the frame.

Plus they spent too much time looking in the mirror instead of at me. I found out they liked mirrors a lot. Even in the bedroom. Plus they were never positioned so I could see anything.

Self centered is what they were, what Freud called narcissistic. I'd been reading *Freud for Everyman* bit by bit, and I had begun to see what made people tick. Sex, power, and money.

Plus maybe some lusting after one parent or the other.

That idea of Freud's had me stumped. How—no, *why*— would I lust after either of them? It was difficult enough just picturing my parents getting slippery for each other. The very thought of those flabby old farts at a petting party or chasing naked through the family homestead put me off my feed for a couple of days.

~~~

WINTER IN CALIFORNIA is like summer most places, with plenty of sunshine, even when the air's a little nippy. And it never snowed! It would rain every so often and the city would grind to a halt, like no one had ever seen water come out of the sky before.

I loved it here because I could always wear dresses with bright colors, not like back East where women muffle themselves in gray and brown for six months. They reminded me of trees that had lost their leaves and gone dormant for the winter.

I worked pretty regular right on through the spring, doing back-up dancing in a string of musicals at RKO and some more bit parts at MGM. One day in June, he who shall be nameless spotted me on the lot and asked if I would have a late supper with him, said he had something to talk over with me.

I had wondered if he was ever going to get around to taking me out again. I had heard that his oh-so-public romance was heating up. But still, isn't variety the spice of life? And anyway I heard she was kind of a prude, despite her exhibitionist tendencies.

See how much Freud I had managed to soak up?

He picked me up about nine that night and took me way out to nowhere, a little jazz club on Seventh Street near the train terminal. The band was hot and most of the folks inside were colored. They didn't seem to mind a white couple taking a table for themselves, and the head waiter knew him, so I guessed he had been there a time or two.

We listened to music and downed some very smooth martinis. After a while we had some Southern fried chicken for a late night supper. It tasted great and I was enjoying myself, but he was preoccupied.

A Negro photographer came by and snapped a photo that caught us unaware. I had a mouthful of chicken and was laughing, but my date went pale. He jumped up and went after the cameraman. They talked together heatedly for a few moments, and then he gave him some bills from his wallet. The photographer pulled the slide from his negative carrier, exposing the film, then handed it to him.

When he got back to the table I asked what that was all about.

"I can't have a photo of us together showing up in some newspaper. Not in some colored club."

"I heard there was no such thing as bad publicity," I said.

"You do know I'm engaged, don't you?"

I gave him knowing smile number four. "Who cares?"

He got up from the table and threw down two twenty- dollar bills, which should have covered our food and drink four times. "Let's go somewhere that we can talk in private."

He drove us to a little motor court on the east side of town. I figured I knew where this was going, so I kept quiet while he checked us in, trying to figure my best angle. He surprised me by fetching a little valise from the rear of his Cadillac V-12.

Once we were inside and the blinds were drawn he opened the valise and pulled out a gorgeous silk nightgown and several scarves. He handed me the nightgown.

"This should fit," he said. "I think you're the same size."

"This is hers?"

He nodded, then stood waiting impatiently. I fingered the nightgown. I've felt spider webs more substantial. I could smell expensive perfume on the fabric. And the scent of another woman underneath that.

"I don't understand," I said.

But I did.

He moved away from me and flicked off the lights. It was darker, but I could still see.

"There are some things—she doesn't like to—she won't let—"

"I'm an actress. I can do her." I slipped off the shoulder straps of my dress and let it fall to the ground. I moved into the yellow puddle of light cast by the streetlamp hitting the blinds. "And once you see how good an actress I am, I expect bigger roles than I've been getting. Understood?"

He was staring at my body, the way a doctor does just before he asks you climb on up there, but he shook his head yes. I took my time while I put on the nightgown, kind of a reverse striptease. When I was covered I went to the bed to turn it down. He came up behind me and looped a scarf around my arm.

That surprised me, but I didn't let it show. I'd had plenty of guys want something a little unusual. As long as it paid off for me, so what? Maybe I'd pick up something new, something I liked. I'd already learned a couple of tricks with knotted silk handkerchiefs like to drive men crazy.

He was all business, not rough, but focused on something only he could see, as he laid me out on the bed and arranged me just so. Once he had my wrists tied to the headboard he used another scarf for my eyes. I heard him undressing.

When I figured he was buck naked I put on my Harlow voice and called out, "Honey? Is that you?" Sultry, you know?

"I have an image in my mind of her lying helpless before me," he said, his voice kind of low, like he had a cold.

I stayed in character. "But darling, I'll do whatever you ask."

"I said helpless, not obedient."

He jammed a wadded-up scarf into my mouth and then bound it in place with another, pulling it painfully tight when I let out a little yelp of protest. Now that I was trussed like a turkey I wasn't sure if I should try to break loose or be as still as possible.

He pulled up the silk nightgown, fluffed it to capture some air, and let it float back down onto my body.

"You're not a natural blond," he said.

After the first blow landed it was a long downhill slide into unconsciousness.

~~~

WHEN I CAME to I found that I wasn't tied up any longer. The scarves and the nightgown were gone. I was stark naked with just a sheet over me.

I tried to sit up. That was a mistake. Pain shot through me like I'd grabbed a live electric wire.

I hurt everywhere. He had really worked me over. I rolled off the bed and got to my knees.

I crawled into the bathroom and pulled myself up using the edge of the sink. I cried when I saw the bruises that covered my body.

Not my face, though. He hadn't hit me there.

It took me a couple of hours to get dressed. I found two hundred dollars and a note that only read "Call me," signed with just his initial.

I telephoned for a cab and got myself home, where I soaked most of the day in a tub full of Epsom salts and cold water. I couldn't walk down to the boulevard for a meal, so I called a Chinese place that would deliver.

I hated to admit it, even to myself. Mama had been right when she warned me that some men were bastards.

I'd believed I knew better. I figured they mostly wanted to have some fun, like me.

I'd just been lucky up till then.

Now some of those passages in Freud that I'd found so mysterious were making sense.

It turns out the forest is a lot darker than I thought.

six~
Making Whoopee
August 1932

IT TOOK MORE than a month for the bruises to fade. As far as I could afford, I dressed like Harlow. I had my dates take me to clubs where she had been seen recently. I had my picture taken with every actor, writer, director, and producer I got near. Some of the photos made the papers, other times it was just a snippet in a gossip column. Sometimes the gossip items confused me with Harlow. I liked that just fine, seeing if I could stir things up.

An agent I dated got me some back-up dancing over at Warner Brothers. He was a nice guy, liked the fact that I looked so much like Harlow with my peroxide job and all. We drove out to a roadhouse in Cucamonga, him being married and not wanting word to get back to the little woman.

"Gayle, I gotta tell you, I'm not sure impersonating Harlow is such a great thing for your career."

"I've had my photo in the *Tattler* twelve times, Barney."

"But the readers don't know it's you."

"What do you mean? My name's right there in the caption," I said, feeling kind of miffed at his criticism. "You're the one always yacking about publicity."

"Folks see your picture, they assume it's Harlow, and never bother to read the caption. You're boosting her career, not yours."

That made me sit up straight. All that work and it wasn't even advancing the stardom I felt was my destiny.

"Can't you get me work as kind of a less expensive sexy blonde, maybe over at Monarch or Republic? You know, sort of Harlow on a budget?"

He took a long pull on his draft beer before he answered.

"I don't think that's gonna happen," he said.

"All right, then, what do you suggest?"

He leered at me, putting his hand over mine.

"I think we ought to sleep on it."

The next morning I woke before Barney did and pocketed his monogrammed silk handkerchief. A girl never knows when some little souvenir might come in handy.

~~~

I PUZZLED OVER how best to get what I wanted, but in the meantime I needed gigs to cover my rent and groceries. I wasn't sharing a room with Jacqueline any more. Too often we had both wanted the place to ourselves to do some entertaining.

I'd found a nice little bungalow in the hills near the entrance to Hollywoodland, up Beachwood a half mile past Franklin. It was cute, and it had a big shade tree to keep the place from getting too hot in the summer.

It was only a few minutes walk to the Red Car line on Hollywood Boulevard.

I didn't blackmail Barney, though I did give it some serious thought. But the more I mulled it over, the more I realized that he didn't have enough dough to make it worth my while. If I wanted real moolah, then I needed to set my sights higher.

Bern and Harlow got married in July and he bought her a swell place in the Hollywood hills, though I heard she wasn't all that keen on it. The "happy couple" was in all the papers, and the MGM publicity machine was working overtime. Ever since Harlow made such a splash with *Red Headed Woman,* they knew she was a milch cow and could make them a barrel of money.

I was going to get my share of that barrel.

That need burned me in all the wrong places, like a dose of the clap.

~~~

THEN ALONG CAME Al Haine. We met during the rehearsal for some fathead's clever idea of a dancing-singing-gangster movie. I drew Al as my partner for a number called the "Tommy Gun Tango." I thought a man that tall would be as graceless as a scarecrow, but I found that he hoofed pretty good.

And that Irish brogue! He could turn it up and down like the flame of a gas burner on the stove.

As to my own accent, he said, "You're not from the British Isles. You sound phony as a three-dollar bill."

"Keep it down, bud. This English bit is what I use to set me apart from all the other gals that have made their way to Hollywood."

"Anyone from across the Atlantic can hear you're

an American pretending to be a Brit. Your accent is too broad."

I gave him a nasty glare. "Everybody's a critic. My gramma said to say nothing at all if you had nothing nice to say."

"Ah, but who would be caring about your accent when you have the face of an angel?"

"That's a much nicer thing to say."

"Have dinner with me and I'll say even nicer things."

We were on a break from the dance rehearsal, backs against the wall of the studio, dripping perspiration from our workout. We drank lemonade—which he improved with a quick splash from his hip flask.

"You dance a wicked tango," said Al. "Makes my heart go giddyup." I made a moue, so he went on. "And you have a body that would make a bishop kick a hole in a stained glass window."

I giggled like a school girl at that one. This guy served blarney by the shovelful. Not that I didn't like it, but I knew it for what it was. (Later I realized I should never have repeated Al's gag to that word-thief Chandler.)

Still, Al had a great smile and made me laugh to beat the band. I thought he might be a candidate to see my dimples.

Two hours later they passed out the tommy guns which figured in the latter part of the dance number. They weren't real, just dummies made out of wood and rubber, but they sure looked dangerous.

"Does anyone here know how to fire this?" said the dance master. Several of the men raised their hands, including Al, though he didn't make a big thing of it like a couple of the guys who were trying to show off.

"I used it plenty in the trenches," said one pretty boy.

Under his breath Al said to me, "The war ended fourteen years ago and he can't be more than twenty-five. What's he playing at?"

The dance master handed him the gun and said to all of us, "Only one of these will be real and it will be loaded with blanks, not bullets, though that's dangerous enough. The rest of yours will have small Roman candles placed inside the barrels, so they throw off jets of sparks. But I need all of you to hear how loud the real one is so that you aren't frightened. I don't want you jumping around like dogs on the Fourth of July. There are only ten rounds loaded, so the firing will last less than a second."

He nodded to Pretty Boy, who put on his best "I am a responsible adult" look, aimed the tommy gun at the ground, and pulled the trigger.

Nothing.

Pretty Boy blinked twice and pulled the trigger several more times. Silence.

Al stepped forward, nodded to the dance master, and took the tommy gun into his own hands. He pulled back on some lever or other, cocking the weapon I guess, and let it rip.

Flame and smoke shot out of the muzzle a good yard. A roar like thunder echoed in the dance studio for seconds after the firing stopped.

All the women dancers and half the men screamed. The dance master looked as if he might faint. After a moment the screamers gave in to nervous laughter.

Al brought the muzzle of the gun near his lips, lazy-like, and blew the smoke away, as if he was putting out a match. He handed the machine gun back to the unnerved dance master.

"That's how it's done," said Al. "You might want to make sure whoever is supposed to fire this actually knows the weapon."

At last I was able to take a breath, shaky as it was.

There's something about a man who can handle his gun.

~~~

AL WAS JUST as capable in other departments as well. We spent a memorable couple of hours trying out our moves on each other, soaking through the sheets with our perspiration.

He was lying there breathing hard, but not yet drifting off, when I went into my tiny kitchen. I got us a nice big glass of gin with ice. I needed to get his attention, but I also wanted him receptive to my idea.

He drank down about half the glass and toasted someone named Colleen, a former girlfriend I suppose. I can't say I cared much for that.

I told him I had some business ideas.

"But first I need to clear something up."

"Yes?" said Al, raising his eyes from my breasts to my face, but only for a moment.

I was facing him on the bed, sitting nude, Indian style. I jerked the sheet over my body.

"I'm up here. And I need your concentration."

"Oh, I was concentrating, sure enough."

"If we're going to do business together I need to be straight with you, and I want you to be straight with me."

Al snickered. "It's a bit soon, but I'm willing to try it again."

I threw the pillow at him and knocked the gin glass from his hand.

"Don't be cute. It hasn't made you rich."

Al picked up the tumbler, plucked out the ice cube that remained stuck at the bottom, and popped it in his mouth. He looked peeved and said, "Don't go thinking you know me, Gayle."

"Let's start right there. My name isn't Gayle Barton-Poole or anything Barton-Poole. It's plain old Jackie Sue. Jackie Sue Palmer."

He looked a question at me.

"I got me a new birth certificate with a more classy name on it because Hollywood is chock full of Jackie Sue's from every hick town in the United States. Being from England and having an accent was my edge, the best way I could stand out from the crowd."

"Jackie Sue, is it?" Al reached across and offered his hand. "Pleased to make your acquaintance." And damned if he didn't smirk.

"So why don't you tell me your real name and where you're from and what you do for a living," I said. "Because you sure aren't a professional dancer."

"There's no need to be insulting myself, Jackie Sue. And my whole name is Aloysius Joseph Lambert Haine. Believe me, I wouldn't make up a moniker like that. I took many a bloody nose over it."

I unclenched my jaw and took a breath. It didn't take long for me to lay out my scheme for generating some quick cash. He listened closely.

"That's when you come through the door and snap a photo of us, me in my sheer negligee and him with his pants around his ankles," I said. "He'll pay cash on the spot to keep his wife from seeing that picture." I looked at Al who had kind of a funny smile. "I need someone your size to make sure he doesn't just smash the camera and rough us up." I paused, waiting for him to can that smile. "All right, what's so funny?"

"You're saying you invented this idea yourself?"

"You don't think a woman is smart enough to plan something like that?" I was beginning to get my Irish up. I reached across for my satin robe and slipped it on, cinching the belt. "Well, maybe the next fella will be more appreciative."

"I don't know exactly how to tell you this, but your idea isn't new. It's so old it has a name: the badger game."

"The badger game? Where'd that come from?"

Al shrugged. "I heard this particular con was very popular in Milwaukee, and Wisconsin's the Badger State, so perhaps that's the source."

I was peeved that he discounted my idea just because it wasn't new. "Doesn't mean it won't work here in Los Angeles."

"You're right." He laughed. "I think this works any place where men fear a charge of adultery in a divorce case."

~~~

IT WAS ANOTHER week before I told Al the rest of my plan. Once we had the technique down, I wanted to get a load of photos with me in full Harlow makeup, each one with a different man. I figured MGM would pay plenty to keep those pix from getting into the tabloids and destroying their rising star.

What I didn't say was that I was just as sure that *he* would see the photos, seeing how high up he was in the hierarchy at Metro. I figured he would have enough of what Freud would call "sexual insecurity" to be jealous. Plus he would feel humiliated about how many other men had seen the snapshots of her fooling around.

That would be my revenge and my secret.

Because I'd been hurt, dammit. It would take cash to make me feel better, like Mama's kiss on a scraped elbow.

MISS ILONA'S
HOLLYWOOD SCRAPBOOK
PART IV: *THOMAS INCE*

HOLLYWOOD'S DAILY TATTLER

FATHER OF THE WESTERN DIES ON HEARST YACHT!

--November 19, 1924

Thomas H. Ince, 42, former partner of D.W. Griffith and Mack Sennett, died of an apparent heart attack while attending his own birthday party aboard the yacht *Oneida*, owned by newspaper magnate William Randolph Hearst.

Other prominent guests in attendance at the untimely event were famed comedian Charlie Chaplin, gossip columnist Louella Parsons, author Elinor Glyn, and rising actress Marion Davies.

MYSTERY SURROUNDS INCE'S DEATH!

--November 25, 1924

Early stories that Ince's heart attack was brought on by a case of indigestion are pure invention. So is the report that an ambulance rushed him from the Hearst ranch in northern California to his family in Los Angeles so he could die surrounded by his loved ones.

A little bird tells us that the first headline for the *Los Angeles Times* read: "Movie Producer SHOT on Hearst Yacht." We understand that the editor who okayed that banner is no longer employed by Hearst Corporation–or employable at any newspaper.

Why are there rumors that Ince was shot in the head? And why was the body cremated so quickly? Why has there been no police inquiry?...

WHO IS BEHIND THE DEATH OF THOMAS INCE?

--December 1, 1924

Daily Tattler understands that Marion Davies angered sugar daddy WRH with her flirtatious behavior at Ince's birthday party. What isn't clear is whether she was flirting with Charlie Chaplin (soon to be father of a child with his 16-year-old costar, Lita Grey) or if she was making eyes at Thomas Ince.

It is known that WRH kept a loaded pistol aboard the *Oneida* and liked to surprise guests with his ability to pick off seagulls that flew alongside the yacht...

SAN DIEGO DA CLOSES INCE "INQUEST"
--March 11, 1925

"Cover up" best describes the ludicrous inquest into Thomas Ince's death. The San Diego District Attorney only bothered to call a single witness, a Dr. Daniel Goodman, an employee of Hearst Corporation. The good doctor testified that Ince complained of chest pains earlier in the day of his demise. Goodman had traveled by train with the director to join the Hearst party aboard the *Oneida*. Ince supposedly told Goodman that he had experienced such pains several times before.

The DA felt that this adequately explained the cause of Ince's death and the inquest was closed!

Daily Tattler says something stinks in Denmark—and San Diego, too.

MARSHAL LAWE REDUX

"For every human problem,
there is a neat, simple solution;
and it is always wrong."
—H. L. Mencken
Prejudices

one~
Club Alabam
August 1932

GLADYS AND I drove over to Club Alabam to pick up her last pay envelope. She'd left two weeks before and hadn't showed her face since. She feared the detective would come back looking for her. We had tried to protect her by not giving a forwarding address to anyone. We knew Aunt Naomi wouldn't say anything to the police except that she had thrown her grand-niece out of the house and didn't know or care where she roosted.

We needed the money for a rental deposit, or I would have just let it go. We were moving in to Miss Ilona's bungalows, and I wasn't leaving any way for Al or the Kipling Hotel to contact me. We both wanted a clean start.

Gladys had finally—and I mean after an all-night discussion and about a bucket of tears from the both of us—had finally agreed to marry me. We'd gotten the license, although she warned me not to look too hard at her identification from New York. The clerk at city hall didn't give it a second glance, just collected our three dollars and said we had ninety days to make use of it.

We got to Club Alabam a bit after nine, parking behind it near the door to the kitchen. I wanted to go in with her, but she said they didn't much care for "a white police" to come poking around.

"Just because you change your clothes don't mean you look like you're in a new line of work," she said.

"A white police is all I am to you?"

She smiled and pecked me on the cheek as she slid out the door.

I let her go inside while I lit up a cigarette and twisted the radio dial, looking for some music. KFI came on good and clear. I was relaxing to some lively jazz when four Negroes came around the side of the building. As soon as they caught sight of me they rushed the car, one pulling a sap from his pocket and another drawing a knife.

I scrambled to get to the pistol I had stashed under my seat, but one of them got hold of my arm and jerked me hard against the door. Another opened the passenger side door and pushed inside, putting his knife to my throat.

"What the hell you think you doin'?" said the one wielding the knife. "You can't shake us down twice in the same night."

I tried to speak but by now there was an arm squeezed around my neck.

The others dragged me out of the car. The smallest of the four took a closer look at the car.

"Look at this. The police decals been sanded off. I think this guy tryin' to con us, pretendin' to be a policeman."

Knife Guy looked at me in disbelief. "You that stupid? Think you can run a con on the LAPD?" He laughed in my face, giving me a shower, and said, "Let's call Detective Joseph and let him deal wif this boy. He have him some fun."

The third guy, who had been quiet so far, kept his silence, preferring to express his disapproval with a quick jab to my solar plexus. I doubled over and retched up my dinner, ended up on my hands and knees. The four of them argued the merits of calling the detective and whether there was some profit to be had from my situation. The one with the sap used it to tap me on the tip of my shoulder, and I went down flat on the ground. It's nigh unbelievable the world of pain something that small can deliver. It felt like a tractor had run over my arm.

That was when Gladys screamed, loud enough to wake the dead. It got their attention all right.

"What happened to Petey?" She rushed over and knelt beside me, putting my head in her lap. "Someone call an ambulance. He doesn't look good." She started in to crying and the four men shuffled a bit.

"You know this pecker—this white man, Gladys?" said Knife Guy.

"He's my fiancé. He drove me down here so I could collect my last pay."

The four of them exchanged looks, then two bent down and grabbed my arms, pulled me to my feet.

"We didn't know he was with you, Gladys. Thought

he was playin' at being a cop, was gonna try to shake down the club."

"The cops already come by for their weekly envelope. The boss thought maybe Vice Squad was gonna try settin' a new collection schedule. He tole us to have a talk wif him."

It took them another two minutes to get me situated in the back seat and apologize to Gladys some more. I didn't say a word, being too busy gritting my teeth to keep from yowling. My arm was numb from shoulder to wrist as a result of the blow of the sap, and I couldn't drive. Gladys took the wheel and got us back to our cottage, where I downed some aspirin and tried to get some sleep.

two~
Beverly Hills

I REPORTED TO work at MGM the next morning, my arm stiff and sore. First break I got, I went over to the paint shop and arranged to get my Ford a quick paint job. The old black and white was doing me too much harm and attracted the wrong kind of attention.

I was able to get Whitey Hendry to authorize the labor at studio expense, since I was going to use the car in the performance of my duties. All I had to do was pay for the paint. Whitey was the head of the MGM police force, though it had no true police authority. Still, he was in tight with the LAPD, and they'd given him a courtesy badge to flash when he wanted access somewhere or to intimidate someone.

My first task of the day was to get over to Beverly Hills and collect one of our contract actresses who had spent the night in the drunk tank. I drove over in a plain sedan with tinted windows in the rear doors.

The actress—I won't mention her stage name—was still drunk and smelled of puke. Her lipstick was smeared and her mascara had run. Her blouse was rucked and something had stained her pencil skirt. In short, she looked like hell.

I took her into an interview room and wiped most of the makeup off, then pulled a scarf over her tangled hair, added sunglasses to hide the red-rimmed eyes, and put an overcoat over the whole mess. Once she was reasonably disguised I took her by the elbow and led her into the corridor.

I snagged a passing officer.

"Her paperwork is already cleared. I have a car parked out back. Can you point us to the rear exit so we can avoid any newshounds might be waiting outside?"

He was annoyed at being interrupted on his way to coffee and doughnuts and was about to snap at me when he did a double take.

"Is that who I think it is?"

I nodded, while she stifled a sulfurous belch.

"I love her pictures."

"And the studio hopes you'll keep on loving them."

He led us to a door that had to be unlocked with a key and we were outside. Even through her sunglasses I could see her blink owlishly while I bundled her into the back seat.

"Laura, stay low. We don't want the press to see you as I come out of the parking lot."

She nodded, then grabbed her head after the movement.

"Aspirin," she whispered hoarsely.

"I don't have any with me. Let me get you to your house and we'll find some for you."

"No aspirin?"

"No."

"Gin. I need gin."

"I don't have any of that with me, either. Besides I think you've had enough. You'll ruin your health if you keep this up."

She snapped her fingers at that, to indicate her contempt for the advice. I pulled out of the rear parking area of the police station, stopping at the driveway to check the traffic. A photographer come from behind a bush and bulled his way up to the car, pressing his Speed Graphic against the car window. A flash went off and Laura groaned.

I hit the gas and we rabbit hopped into the near lane. The cameraman called out to his buddies that there was a star in my car and several more came toward us. I floored it and spun the wheel, squealing across two lanes as I made a U-turn.

The sharp turn threw Laura across the back seat and she fetched up with a bump against the other door. I checked the rearview mirror, saw no one following, then looked to check on the actress. I couldn't find her in the mirror, so I turned my head and threw a quick glance over the back seat.

Laura picked that moment to vomit copiously onto the floor. After a moment the smell hit me, and I thought I was going to lose my lunch as well. I rolled down the window and picked up speed.

I spent a half hour driving to her house, fifteen minutes getting her into the house, and ten minutes finding the aspirin and getting it into her, before I was able to leave her moaning into her sofa cushions. I took one of her guest towels, swabbed out the floorboards of the car, and threw the towel onto her porch. Probably did her a favor, keeping solicitors away.

I made my way back to the studio. With luck I could spend the rest of the day fixing parking tickets. Studio executives seemed to think they could leave their cars wherever they pleased and for as long as they wanted, no matter how the street was posted.

~~~

GLADYS WAS WORKING days that week, so we had the evening together. We made plans for each of us to take Friday off, go down to city hall, and make it legal.

"You're not getting cold feet, are you?" she said.

"I'm expecting you to keep 'em warm."

And she did.

Later, when we were just talking, sitting comfortably on the old sofa we'd had delivered from a secondhand store, she told me stories of old Hollywood. Some of them made me wonder that they hadn't outlawed the whole motion picture business years ago.

"So you're telling me that Charlie Chaplin maybe shot and killed a studio owner?"

"Seems like it had to be him or William Randolph Hearst, and it happened on Hearst's yacht."

"I would have thought I'd have read something about Charlie being involved in murder."

"The studios and the cops are pretty good at hushing things up, 'specially if it's bad for business."

"Where you getting all this information?"

"Our landlady, Miss Ilona, is a big fan of the movies. She keeps scrapbooks about the doings of the famous," said Gladys. "Lot of her stories come from a newspaper called *The Hollywood Tattler.*"

"That's not a newspaper. It's just a scandal sheet."

"Well, maybe it's not a newspaper you like to read, but

those stories are in print. If they wasn't true, the people being talked about would sue them, most likely."

I reasoned to myself that this discussion was going no place good. So I pulled Gladys' feet into my lap and began to rub them. Every waitress I ever talked to complained that her feet hurt.

Gladys was too smart for that.

"Don't you go thinking a foot rub is the way to change the topic of conversation."

"I never had any such thought," I said, dead serious.

And we both busted out laughing.

So of course that's when the telephone rang. The thing had only been installed for two days, and hardly anyone kenned we were living in LA, much less knew our telephone number.

I answered and talked with my boss for a couple of minutes. When I hung up, I let out a sigh and went to get fully dressed.

"Maybe we shouldn't have got that device," I said. "Now they can call me out for an errand any time of day or night."

"You want I should come along?"

"Not with you serving breakfast at the restaurant first thing in the morning. I'm likely to be late on this one. Seems one of the studio's rising stars got into a fight out on that gambling ship, the *Johanna Smith*. He busted some businessman in the jaw and Mr. Businessman wants the cops to arrest him for assault and battery. I need to go out there, calm folks down, and get our boy under wraps so the press don't get wind of it."

Gladys wasn't happy about me going out, and neither was I, but we needed the paycheck.

three~
Johanna Smith

I GOT DOWN to Long Beach about half past eight, then had to wait for a water taxi to take me out to the ship. There were plenty of people in a party mood waiting alongside me. Most of them were dressed to the nines, and I saw that standing next to them I looked like a plainclothes cop. Which I kinda was.

An unmarked van pulled up to unload cases of what surely had to be bottles of beer. A Negro did the heavy lifting, and I thought I recognized him. I would have gone over to make sure, but it came to me that it was no longer any of my business where alcoholic beverages came from or went to.

I'm not big on traveling by boat. Three point one miles out to sea, just getting past the limit of state jurisdiction, bouncing along the late-night swells didn't make me any happier about it. The only thing of interest was the occasional flying fish springing out of the phosphorescent wake of the boat, which I wouldn't have believed if I didn't see it with my own eyes.

I hung back as the rest of the guests boarded the ship. Finally it was just me and the guys ready to bring up the cases of beer. An officer of the ship, looking pretty sharp in his uniform—could have been an admiral with all the gold braid he had on—came over and asked what I was up to. He brought two beefy bouncers with him.

"MGM sent me over to fetch one of our actors. I understand he mixed it up with another of your guests. Studio wants me to soothe your other guest and get my guy out of town, without the cops being involved."

"So that wasn't a complete fabrication, he really is an actor?" The admiral gave a look to the bouncers, who turned without a word and disappeared into the bowels of the ship.

"It's going to take a few minutes for the boys to get him out of the brig. He was quite obstreperous. In the meantime, why don't I show you around? I'll introduce you to the other guest in question. Maybe you can buy him a drink. We don't care to gain a reputation that would discourage guests from visiting regularly."

I'd been to gambling dens before but I'd never seen a setup like this. There must have been fifty slot machines, plus roulette wheels, craps tables, blackjack, and bingo. There was a small area for poker where the house did all the dealing. A small combo played at the other end of the room where couples were dancing, moving between the casino and the open air of the deck.

A full bar had its row of customers, but I saw a number of bargirls serving the gamblers at their games. I also spied one of the girls cut a deal with a man in a tuxedo and lead him through some doors at the side, off to a private room, I assumed.

The smoke was thick enough to cut with a knife, a

bunch of it coming from fat Cuban cigars. When I got a glimpse of the stakes on the roulette table, I knew I was way out of my league, not that I had any great desire to gamble. But I do have to say that there was excitement in the air, and folks seemed to be having a good time.

The admiral touched a middle-aged gent at the roulette table on the arm and he spun around looking belligerent. He had the makings of nice bruise on his jaw. I was introduced to Mr. Stokely, and I asked if I could have a chat with him at the bar, buy him a drink.

He looked me over and I believe he thought I was the policeman he'd been asking for. In any case, he allowed as how I could buy him some brandy.

He nodded to a busty redhead in a lamé gown cut dangerously low and said, "I'll be back shortly, my dear. I expect to find you in the same place I left you."

We went to the bar and he ordered the most expensive brandy they carried. The studio had given me a hundred bucks to keep on me to take care of the various gratuities I had to pay out in the course of my duties, so I slapped a ten spot down to pay for the drink. I made sure he caught a glimpse—but not too close a look—at my courtesy badge from the studio.

I assured him that it was in all our interests to let this matter drop. The casino owners didn't want a reputation as a dangerous place for guests, the police didn't want to have to shut down a place that provided such sought-after entertainment so near our coast, and the guests didn't want to lose their source of amusement. I said I'd arrange to get him a hundred-dollar line of credit at the table of his choice.

He snorted at the mention of a hundred dollars. I should have guessed that was the wrong amount by looking at the cut of his clothes and the price of his mistress. I tried a different tack.

"Is there some other problem I can solve for you?"

"The problem is that fool was flirting with my—niece— and she was naïve enough to respond to his attentions. He claimed he was a movie star and she fell for his line."

I blinked at that. He was pretending the girl was his niece, for crying out loud. And he didn't recognize the actor himself. I bought him another brandy and he mellowed enough to let me escort him back to the roulette table. His "niece" was chatting amiably with a stunning brunette, her hair cut in a fashionable bob, wearing a diamond choker and pendant that dazzled my eyes at the same time it drew my gaze deep into her cleavage. She probably had a dress on, too, but I had lost track somehow.

The redhead looked up as we approached and turned the brunette to face Stokely.

"Uncle! Can you believe it? It's my roommate from college, Colette Spears! But we all called her Coco. Coco, this is my Uncle Andy."

"You never told me your uncle was so handsome," cooed Coco.

Uncle Andy forgot all about me as the two women each took one of his arms and he began fantasizing about a threesome. With one part of my task accomplished, I turned and headed for the door when a hand clasped my arm.

"Marshal! I thought I'd lost ye, but now here you are."

And there was Al Haine, big as life and still red haired. Now, though, instead of the scruffy clothes that looked as if they'd been taken off a scarecrow, he was wearing a crisp tuxedo and patent leather shoes.

He shook my hand till I feared I might lose circulation in it. I had the sense he was steering me away from someone or something, so of course I cast a glance over my shoulder.

And caught a wink from Coco, directed at Al. It all snapped into place for me. There was some con going on.

Al saw that I was onto him.

"Hang on a moment while I gather my winnings," he said as he scraped a wad of cash from the table. My mouth must have dropped open as I estimated how much he gathered in, because he added. "Luck of the Irish, to be sure." He guided me away from the table toward the door to the deck. "We need to catch up. I've been wondering what came of ye."

"Much as I'd like to talk, I have to meet someone, Al. I'm here on business and I'll be leaving soon."

"I was about to catch the water taxi meself. I'll wait for you and we'll chat on the way to shore."

I saw it wouldn't be easy to shake him, so I arranged to meet him in ten minutes. I found the admiral and asked after my wayward actor. He pointed to a disheveled figure sitting on a coil of rope in the shadows, wrapped in a blanket. I went over and put my hand on his shoulder. The man shuddered away from me.

"Johnny, the studio sent me to help get you home. You've caused enough trouble tonight."

When he looked up and the light caught his face, I saw the bouncers had worked him over pretty good. Black eye, mashed nose, a split lip, a cut on his forehead. I offered him a hand and he came to his feet, grunting in pain. He hobbled over to the gangplank and stood with his back to me. I decided I'd try to give the kid some advice I wish someone had given me at his age.

"No matter how tough you think you are, there's always someone even tougher," I said. "Looks like you met one of them."

"Took more than one of them to do this to me," he mumbled.

I saw he didn't care for education or philosophy, so I left him to his thoughts. Al sauntered up and the admiral blew a shrill note on a whistle, and we all three got onto the bobbing water taxi, along with an elderly gent accompanied by his "grand-niece," no doubt. Johnny hunkered in a corner by himself, so Al had my undivided attention and kept up a line of chatter as we made our way to shore.

He did tell me something pretty interesting, though.

"I met a member of the LAPD Vice Squad, Marshal. I believe the City of the Angels might be better named City of Fallen Angels."

"How's that?"

"I'm not a man taken by statistics, but this has the nature of a poem. He gave me to understand that Los Angeles is home to eighteen hundred bookies, six hundred bordellos, and three hundred gambling dens housing more than twenty thousand slot machines. He didn't even include the ten pleasure ships moored off the coast here."

"Those are the numbers he told you?" I said. "Why would he tell you that? Makes it seem like the Vice Squad ain't doing much of a job, don't it?"

"Well, he was in his cups and had misplaced his better

judgment. He was bragging about the fine living he was making from LA vice."

"On the take, I suppose."

"I believe that's the term for it. At least it was in Chicago."

"And how'd you come to be talking to him?"

"I was after presenting the men in blue with a case of the finest as a gift from the boys at the dog track. They concluded a most successful season, and I had participated profitably."

"You're a wonder, Al."

So, after that I had to tell him about my jobs in the western movies and how I was working security at MGM now.

"Say, did you ever find that gal from Peony Springs, the one who moved out here?" Al looked smug. "You know, the one you weren't really following." Damned if he didn't laugh at me, though it seemed to be good natured.

"Yes, yes, I did. As a matter of fact Gladys and I are tying the knot this Friday down at city hall."

"You don't say so. This calls for a celebration. Once we're ashore I happen to know of a certain establishment where we can find something to imbibe."

"Much as I'd like to, I have to get this guy," I jerked a thumb at the morose actor, "to a studio doctor and make sure the press don't catch sight of him looking like a piece of hamburger. Maybe another time."

Al wasn't to be put off that easily. "So who's standing up for youse?"

"What to do you mean?"

"If it's a civil ceremony you're having, then there need to be two witnesses."

"I thought city hall took care of everything."

"You're a country mouse in the big city, Marshal. I'll be happy to stand up for ye. And I'll bring my colleen along to stand up for your Gladys."

"I don't believe Gladys would take kindly to having Coco as our witness."

"Coco? Oh, you mean the buxom brunette back on board. That's not her real name. And she's merely an associate of mine, just business. I'll be bringing along Gayle, as comely an article as has ever captured my heart."

"Captured your heart, eh? Must be something in the air out here."

"Los Angeles is a glorious place."

And so it was arranged that Al and his colleen would be our witnesses.

GLADYS REVISITED

"Out of the night that covers me,
Black as the pit from pole to pole,
I thank whatever gods may be
For my unconquerable soul."
—*William Ernest Henley*
"Invictus"

one~
City Hall
August 1932

AS IT HAPPENED, I was the one who got the cold feet about getting married. By lunchtime Thursday I thought I was going to faint, and my stomach was rolling around like I'd et some bad fish.

I took the afternoon off and rode the trolley down to my Aunt Naomi's. I wanted her either to give me her blessing or talk me out of marrying Petey, I wasn't sure which.

I should have known better. Asking advice of my oldest relative means hearing the history of the entire family, with an emphasis on the numerous white sheep, so to speak.

Eventually she wound down her recounting of the no-counts, the shiftless, and the feckless twigs on our family tree; about the travails and troubles that had plagued her life beginning with being born into slavery, through marrying three men who lacked proper spines, which was obvious because they up and died on her; the way her body had betrayed her by growing old and shapeless, with her hair and teeth falling out; her arthur-itis, rheumatiz, lumbager, the sugars, corns, and shingles; the ungratefulness of her children, grand-children, nieces, nephews, grand-nieces, grand-nephews, sons-in-laws, daughters-in-laws, and leech-like cousins; the situation in Europe, the Depression, and the need for a Pentecostal revival to save the world; the criminal who was LA's chief of police, our racist mayor, and the idjit in the White House; and door to door salesmen who always rang the bell just as she was in the middle of her bathroom business.

"Girl, I think you been losing your mind, wanting to marry a police. And a white boy, beside."

I understood then. Petey had two strikes against him, and the bigger one was being an ex-cop. She needed to learn a few things about him, and I was just the one to teach her.

"Auntie, you don't know Petey's heart like I do. Back in Peony Springs he was the one standing up to the KKK. He was the one who made sure the town folk didn't go after Darnell when that little white girl run off. If they'd caught my cousin, they'd have lynched him."

She just dribbled into her spit cup and loaded another pinch of Garrett Sweet and Mild.

"Darnell. Hmmph. That boy comin' to no good end. Police come to my door two day ago. I thought they here to search the house again, cuz you brung that trouble on my head. But no, they was lookin' for Darnell. When I let him stay under my roof three year ago he was fool enough to list this as his home address. Now I hear he running whiskey and God know what all for that Uncle Anton."

I couldn't believe my ears. "How do you know about Uncle Anton?"

"He the nephew of Missus Washington in my women's Wednesday night Bible study group. I be prayin' for him to come to Jesus for nigh unto twenty year now. That boy ain't right. One time he have the nerve to come here, right to my home, and say he need to hide something beneaf the floor, in the craw space, say his aunt tell him I wouldn't mind. I tole him I knew his auntie never said no such thing. Tole him if he tell lies like that then his heart be as black as his skin."

I saw Aunt Naomi in a new light. "You called out a gangster to his face?"

"That boy goin' to Hell, and that for sure. He sez to me 'I wouldn't be so uppity about *my* black face. You 'bout ten minutes to midnight youself.' Talkin' back to his elders like that. Goin' to Hell too good for him." And she spat into her can hard enough to make a splash.

I took a breath. If I wanted something, I was going to have to ask her direct.

"Aunt Naomi, you're my oldest living kin, and I'd like you to come see us married down at city hall."

"Won't do it."

"You're going to make me cry, Auntie." And I did start crying, though I tried not to.

She looked at me with some kindness in her eyes. "I can see you love this man, so I guess you goin' to do this anyway. And I hope he make you happy and you make him happy. But I still ain't goin'. Best you not start married life by bringin' me down and causin' talk with his friends and kin."

~~~

I HAVE TO say that Petey and I made a good-looking couple. Not movie star good-looking, but real people good-looking. Petey had his suit pressed with sharp creases in his trouser legs, his boiled shirt just glowing white, a nice burgundy tie, with a matching handkerchief in his breast pocket, and his fedora freshly blocked. I had a new frock with short angel bell sleeves in a nice burgundy jersey that clung in all the right ways, and I had found a pair of ghillies in a matching color that made my feet feel wonderful. I only wished they could be worn at the restaurant.

We were waiting at the Registrar's Office, and though Petey said he wasn't nervous, he paced pretty constant. I don't know if you've been there, but the Los Angeles City Hall is built to large scale, and the hallways are long enough that people disappear in the distance.

Of a sudden he froze looking down the hall, as if he recognized someone.

I followed his glance and saw a tall gangly redhead loping toward us, a petite platinum blonde trailing much further behind, hindered by her four-inch spike heels and tight skirt.

"Halloooo!" called the redhead, waving and smiling. He had on a tailor-made suit that would have cost Petey a month's salary.

"That's Al for you," said Petey. "Likes to make a grand entrance."

And then Petey's voice sort of died away as he stared at the distant blonde.

"Is that who I think it is?" said Petey.

I looked, but my eyes aren't good at distance. I could tell it was a young woman and that's all.

Al was upon us. He shook Petey's hand and put his arm around me and kissed my cheek in what I thought a very forward manner. He'd already had a drink or two if I'm any judge, and his manner was expansive.

"Sorry to keep you waiting, Gladys. I thought Gayle would never finish with the makeup, though she hardly needs it. Even so, she could never match the bride's love-liness."

Oh really, I thought, and gave Petey the fish eye. Petey wasn't paying attention. His eyes were glued to the approaching blonde and I began get my dander up.

"You'll be shaming the sun and the sky," continued Al. With his brogue and his endless line of compliments I knew he was Irish born and bred.

"I can't believe it," said Petey. "Jackie Sue!" he called to the blonde.

The woman froze in place. For that matter, so did I. And Al stumbled over his blarney.

"Not so loud, Marshal. She goes by Gayle now," said Al. "How do you know her real name?"

"So she really did make it to Hollywood," I said.

At last Jackie Sue reached us. She stared at Petey and me and blushed deeply. It was an alarming shade of red set against her platinum blonde hair. She turned on Al.

"You didn't tell me it was Marshal Lawe. I thought your friend's name was Marshall."

Al looked at the expressions on our faces.

"Oh, you're already acquainted then? What a fine

coincidence that is. Hard to believe now, isn't it?"

"Jackie Sue, I never thought I'd ever see you again," I said. "Except on the big screen, of course."

"And I never expected to see either of you two in the rest of my life," said Jackie Sue. "I took you for the type that was like to stay put in their home town until they died." She knew that didn't sound nice. "I didn't mean it that way. It's just such a surprise to meet you here in Los Angeles."

"Seems to me half the country is moving to LA," said Petey. "Either they want to be in the movies or they just like the thought of warm winters and oranges."

"What a fine thing for a wedding," said Al. "Having an old friend on hand watching the two of you tie the knot."

The word wedding made Petey start, and he pulled the license from his inner pocket, and took a look at the signature lines for the witnesses.

"Say, Al, can you step aside for a minute? I have something to ask you," said Petey. The two of them went down the hallway to a drinking fountain, and I could see Petey gesturing pretty widely, with Al making patting gestures as he tried to calm him. I wondered what that could be about.

I turned to Jackie Sue. "That's a beautiful dress. And I didn't recognize you at first because you changed your hair color. You know, you look a lot like that blonde actress, Jean something."

"Harlow. Jean Harlow. Yes, I know I do." She hesitated. "What made the two of you move to Los Angeles?"

"I came out a year and half ago, after my diner was foreclosed by the bank. Moved in with my great-aunt and got a job cooking at a restaurant."

"Sorry to hear your diner went bust. I never did get a chance to eat there. What about Marshal Lawe?"

"So many people left Peony Springs that they decided to move the county seat to a bigger town. And they closed down the marshal's office and Petey was laid off."

"Petey?"

"That's what I call him. He doesn't like his other nicknames."

She nodded and conversation lagged. I could see something was bothering her and she finally got to it.

"Say, do you know how my folks are doing?"

"Don't you stay in touch?"

"After I changed my name I didn't want them coming to fetch me, so I never included a return address when I wrote. I haven't heard anything in a couple of years."

"They lost their farm before my diner was foreclosed. Last I knew, they were living in an apartment over the bakery. Your mother was taking in laundry, and your father was doing handyman work, when he could find it."

She blanched when she heard how hard times were for them.

"What about my brothers?"

"I think they're both still in school, but nowadays I don't have any contact back there myself."

The men came back, Al looking a little on edge. He whispered something to Jackie Sue. She nodded.

"Jackie Sue will be signing the witness line as Gayle Barton-Poole," said Al. "She has a valid ID for that name. It's her stage name."

The Registrar's assistant beckoned us from the door and we went inside.

A dyspeptic Justice of the Peace read the wedding service like it was the phone book, massaging the third button of his waistcoat the whole time. Al beamed at us, enjoying the rite, while Jackie Sue—I mean Gayle—looked thoughtful.

Before you know it, Petey and I were Mr. and Mrs. Lawe. All four of us plus the Justice signed the marriage certificate.

Once we were out on the sidewalk, Al said, "I've taken the liberty of arranging a table at a place I know."

"Uh oh," said Petey to me in an undertone. "You have no idea how much he can drink or the mayhem that seems to follow him around."

But it would have been plain rude not to accept his hospitality, so we let him lead us to a nice place that served clear gin in water glasses, as well as champagne from bottles labeled as carbonated grape juice. I have to say "Gayle" held her liquor well and helped curb Al's excesses.

I did get a good laugh out of his wedding toast.

"May God not weaken your hand," he said. "May we be alive at this same time again."

"What does that mean, Al?" said Jackie Sue. "Say it in plain English."

Al wrinkled his brow as he sought to translate the Irish sentiment. "Means we should all celebrate again on their anniversary."

I was two drinks past my usual limit by this time. "What a good idea! We should do this every year. And at your anniversary, too."

That got a laugh from Jackie Sue and a funny smile from Al.

He raised his glass once more: "May you live long and may you wear it out," he said, casting a glance sideways at Petey.

"Hear, hear!" I said. "Let's open another bottle of that fizzy stuff!"

Later that night I did my best to make the second half come true.

ALOYSIUS RISING

"He has all the virtues I dislike
and none of the vices I admire."
—*Winston Churchill*

one~
Nuptials
August 1932

MARSHAL—OR PETEY, as I now called him—was
a good man. Smart enough to run a small police
department, but not too clever. Honest enough for my
purposes, but not above seeing where his fortune lay. And
ambitious enough that he had found himself working at
the very place where I needed inside information. We were
bobbing along the ocean returning from the *Johanna Smith*,
when he had told me that he was in security at MGM. I
could scarce contain my joy.

I turned my enthusiasm to advantage and made plans
to be his witness when he married the elusive Gladys. I
needed this friendship to bloom. And it couldn't but help
if Gayle became friendly with his missus.

The weather was fair that Friday. In fact, it had been
fair every day since I had been in Los Angeles. Perhaps

it was a drought, but I'd heard no one complain about lack of rain as they did with such irritating regularity in Chicago. I wondered if such brilliant weather would ever become boring.

No sooner had Gayle and I met up with the blessed couple at city hall than I discovered that the three of them knew each other and had all come from the same town in Massachusetts. I realized then that Gayle—I guess I'll just call her by her given name of Jackie Sue—had always been vague about what her home town was, and it soon became clear as to why.

Petey pulled me aside for a man-to-man talk.

"I'm sure she hasn't told you, Al, but Jackie Sue's a runaway. Left her family near three years ago."

"What does it matter? I'd have been a runaway meself if I'd had the sense God gave a donkey."

From the look of him, Petey didn't think I was taking this seriously.

"If you get caught with her, it's a statutory rape charge. She's only sixteen. Well, maybe seventeen; I forget when her birthday is exactly."

I fear my disbelief must have shown.

"I'm telling you, she's had her figure since she was thirteen. Every boy in three counties was sniffing after her." He could see he wasn't getting through to me. "Plus her parents are still looking for her, although considering how much trouble she stirred up when she was living at home, they may not be looking too hard."

I considered the possibilities. "In the worst of cases I'd plead ignorance of her true age, since she showed me her birth certificate."

"She showed you her birth certificate?"

"You know, the one that says she was born in England as Gayle Barton-Poole."

"I'm not sure she can sign our wedding certificate as a legal witness at sixteen."

"You're a born pessimist, Petey."

He cringed a little at hearing his voorneen's pet name for him in my mouth. I led the way back to the Registrar's waiting room.

~~~

I SHOULD HAVE known better, me thinking Jackie Sue was all business, and with a sensual appetite that matched my own. Still, you can't take a young woman—and now I knew exactly how young and impressionable—a young woman to a wedding, no matter how simple it was and stripped of glamour, without her getting stars in her eyes.

"I wonder if I'll ever get hitched," she said to me the next morning. "I mean, me being damaged goods and all."

My head was pounding from the night before, but I'd sworn to myself I wouldn't swallow any hair of the dog till noon.

"I thought you were going to be a star," I said. "Movie stars seem to get their pick of men to marry. From my experience in Hollywood so far, I'm doubtful any of them are virginal." I gave her a big smile. "To be sure, I'm taking a survey, and I'm trying to get as many samples as possible."

We were sitting over breakfast and she gave me a glare that scorched my toast.

"Seems likely I'll wind up with someone who has as damaged a reputation as I do," she said.

BRANT RANDALL AND BRUCE COOK

I felt some unease at this, so I said nothing, just champed the eggs and bacon in front of me.

"Isn't Petey about your age, Aloysius?"

I knew I was in for it now.

"I believe we are the same age, yes."

"And he's settling down now. With nothing more than a steady paycheck and a used police car."

"They're both the bravest of souls, and optimists to boot. Two of the best, trying their best, and I wish them the best."

I was babbling and I knew it. Jackie Sue clicked her fingernails against the table top.

"Whereas you and I have some three thousand dollars between us and are about to make several thousand more," she said. "Plus we're both full of ideas for making money. Our future looks pretty good, I'd say."

"We do have a lot of talent," said I. "And bright prospects."

"Now Gladys is nice enough, but she doesn't compare in the looks department. I'm not trying to be vain here. Just an honest appraisal."

"No question about it. You are the most beautiful thing I've ever seen. No one compares to you. If there were any justice in this world, you would already have been made Queen—"

"Can the malarkey."

She stared into my eyes with a terrible intensity, and I felt the sweat break out upon my brow. Though that could have just been my morning head. It had been a considerable binge we were after having the night before.

"So what's holding you back, Aloysius? Are you already married and you've just been using me? You been stringing me along until something better shows up? Do you think you're going to get more handsome as you get older? I mean, you're already thirty-two, and how much longer do you think your looks will last, before you start to get a gut on you, and your hair begins to thin, and your joints start to creak? You're no bargain today, but I hate to think about five years from now."

I feared she'd go on and on and on.

"Will ye marry me?" I croaked.

She blinked thrice and sat back in her chair. Her silence stretched into a minute, whilst I perspired profusely.

"I'll think about it," she said.

~~~

WE WERE AFTER working the badger game assiduously, sticking with low-level studio executives from all the majors: Fox, Paramount, RKO, Warners, Columbia, even Disney. We stayed away from MGM since that might queer the sting.

It was close to the end of summer and the movie crowd anticipated the big box office that Labor Day weekend usually brought. Workers on the studio lots were excited as well, because big box office meant the start of more projects. Low-level and mid-level executives often received raises when the BO (as *The Daily Variety* called box office receipts) was boffo. Actors and actresses all knew that if their picture made good BO, they could renegotiate their salary skyward.

In short, it was a time of optimism. The economy of the country and the world might lie in ruin, but the motion picture business was thriving. All this came to pass by letting the average person escape their feelings of misery, and for less than a quarter of a dollar.

Jackie Sue and I figured MGM would pay a pretty

penny not to have scandal disrupt the flow of cash being earned by Harlow for the company.

I had a chance to talk with Petey one afternoon as I came to seek background work at MGM. I kept up my extra work at all the studios because it let me spy out likely targets for our con. In truth, I myself needed no more than my gambling skills to pay the rent and buy the groceries, but Jackie Sue and I were close to a payoff large enough to change our lives.

"What brings you out here, Al?"

"They cancelled *Tommy Gun Tim*, the all-singing, all-dancing gangster-musical that the both of us were toiling on over at Warners. Some bigwig finally had the sense to see it was an unprofitable combination."

"Sorry to hear you lost the job. Looked to me like your winnings on the gambling ship should tide you over, though."

"That's not how Jackie Sue sees it. She's pegged her hopes on walking the aisle and having the little cottage with a white picket fence."

"Sharing it with you, I suppose?" said Petey, with a smile so smug I wanted to smack him. "I can't recommend married life too highly. It's good for your soul."

"Words of wisdom, I'm sure. What is it, two weeks now you've been married?"

Petey just laughed. "Come on over to the commissary. I'll treat you to a piece of pie, give you a chance to ogle the starlets."

We ambled across the lot, and along the way I peeked into a dressing room where the door was ajar. A line of dancers looked as if they only had one costume to share between them. Sure and life was grand.

"Whatever happened to the bozo you brought back

from the gambling ship?" I said. "Did they cancel his contract?"

Petey's face clouded a bit. "No, but they fined him, and he won't be able to work until the plastic surgeon can repair his nose and lip."

"Did the press ever catch him looking like Max Schmeling's sparring partner?"

"The idiot left his apartment to buy a newspaper, and a photographer snapped one of him. Cost the studio five thousand to buy the negative."

And that was all I needed to know.

two~
The Ambassador Hotel
September 4, 1932

JACKIE SUE GOT a call from him to come to the restaurant of the Ambassador Hotel at eight p.m. We both deliberated about it, whether or not it was safe to meet him.

"What could he be after?" I said.

"If he wants another session like the last one, he's got another think coming."

"What else could it be?"

"It's not a problem, Al. Take a table nearby and have a drink. If there's going to be trouble, I'll give you the high sign."

We could think of nothing to do but have Jackie Sue meet him and see what was up. She wriggled into a wonderful black cocktail dress, with a fetching short cape over her shoulders. I considered things and decided to slip my Beretta pocket pistol into my suit coat.

We took separate cabs to the Ambassador to keep him from seeing us together. Aye, and it was fortunate we did, because his driver dropped him off just as Jackie Sue's cab pulled up beneath the awning.

I paid my cabbie and went in thirty seconds behind them. For five bucks the maitre d' seated me two tables away. I couldn't hear, but I had no problem seeing if things were to go wrong.

They ordered drinks, and he must have told a joke, because I heard Jackie Sue's laughter, sharp as razor blades, above the clinking of the other diners' silverware. I ground my teeth and nursed my drink.

Ten minutes later he passed her something small and got up from the table. Jackie Sue appeared surprised. He left money to cover their check and walked away without looking back. Jackie Sue watched him go with an odd expression on her face. She took another two minutes to finish her drink and then left the restaurant.

I followed soon after and found her waiting for me.

"He's gone?"

"His driver had the car idling nearby."

"What was it—?"

"Let's get home. This is something we need to discuss in private."

~~~

SHE SPREAD THE cash from the envelope he had handed her on the dinette without saying a word.

"Looks like a thousand to me," I said.

"Yeah. Our last meeting had been on his conscience. Said he understood why I hadn't called him back. Told me he wanted to make things right."

"This is to ease his guilty conscience?"

"I'm also never to call him or try to see him, ever again. He wanted a complete break."

"Does it make sense to you? Because I can't see any."

She shook her head. "Something fishy is going on, but I can't make heads nor tails of it."

We added the thousand to our stash, which was up to six grand now.

"What did he say to make you laugh the way you did?"

"He said, 'These folks need to think we're enjoying each other's company. Laugh as if I'd said something witty.' So I tried."

It was noon the next day that we heard about Harlow's husband.

And then things really moved fast.

JACKIE SUE REPLAYED

"Glory is fleeting
but obscurity is forever."
—*Napoleon*

one~
Making Hay, Getting Mowed
August 1932

AL AND I had done a good job with our badger game, never being greedy, not hitting the same mark twice, moving the con all over the Los Angeles basin. Al spent some time with a photographer learning how to work the Speed Graphic, the camera every news photographer and private detective used. That training paid off, and Al added a nice twist to the game.

The negative carrier for a Speed Graphic had two sides. Normally you pulled out a slide, exposed the film on that side, put the slide back in, and turned the carrier over to expose the second piece of film on the back side. The gag was that most nobody had ever seen any camera but their own Kodak pocket model and had no idea how a newsman's camera worked.

So Al would snap a picture of me and the john through

the window—or from the closet, if we could set it up ahead of time. I got to be good at putting on a negligee in front of the guy and then having him undress while I watched. Al always tried to capture the action just after the mark had dropped his shorts.

Next came the confrontation, the buying of the negative, yak yak yak, and finally Al makes a big show as he rips out the negative carrier, pulls the slide—and gives the bozo a piece of unexposed film, keeping the real negative for ourselves.

By now we had a nice collection of shots that seemed to show Jean Harlow with sixteen different men in sixteen separate locations. We had a choice to make.

We could make a nice score with the tabloids, which would boost their sales far beyond what they might be willing to pay us and probably end Harlow's career. I imagined that I would be able to step into her shoes and continue where she'd left off.

Or we could make up a set of prints, get them delivered to Louis Mayer's home and send a note offering to sell him the negatives. With the cash MGM was earning from her pictures, we figured they'd be willing to pay a hundred grand, easy. For me, the downside was that I wouldn't get to take her parts because she'd still have them.

Al and I talked over which way to go day after day. And then we argued about it night after night. Making up got to be harder and harder for me.

At last Al said this: "Jackie Sue, it's you I am believing in. In my heart I know you can act rings around Harlow. Look at the performance that you put on to snare these marks. It has the touch of genius. And heaven knows you have the sex appeal. These shots of you in the negligee are works of art."

"I hear a 'but' coming."

"But what do we know about the fillum business? Let's find out who the top talent scout is. We'll go and have a screen test, get him to tell us if you have a real future there."

It was all so damn reasonable that I popped him in the eye for it. He cocked his fist to let me have it, but calmed down when I reminded him I still needed my screen test.

~~~

I WOUND UP over at Educational Studio talking with Charles Lamont. He might not have been the top talent scout, but it still cost me two hundred bucks to get a private screen test, which seemed pretty steep to me. I hadn't let Al come along because I thought he might jinx me.

First, I told Lamont about all the small roles I'd had at the various poverty row studios. Then he had his cameraman light me and take some stills. Close shots of my profile, full front, three quarter, looking back over my shoulder, serious, smiling, laughing.

The cameraman had nothing but nice things to say. He was a skinny little guy with a pencil-thin mustache. He loved touching my face as he positioned me so that the light would be just right.

"The camera's going to love you, I can tell," he said "Your skin is great, no bumps or divots. Good bone structure, too. No pouches under your eyes." He leaned close to whisper to me. "How old are you really?"

I just gave him a smile.

Lamont gave me a scene to work on. I spent fifteen minutes memorizing my lines.

"Miss Barton-Poole, are you ready for a run through?" said Lamont. "I'll have Edwin stand next to the camera, which I've positioned as if we're doing the big close-up that would cap the scene. He'll read his lines and you perform to him, but with your eyes looking to this spot here. I've marked it with a bit of tape next to the lens. Do you understand?"

I'd never had any real coaching as an actor from any of the directors I'd worked with, so this was pretty new to me, but all I said was "Sure."

I was excited and nervous at the same time.

Edwin was an actor I recognized from a dozen poverty row westerns. He always played second or third banana. Good looking enough, but didn't have a heroic profile, if you know what I mean. But he was a professional actor, and he did his stuff.

We ran through the scene twice, Edwin feeding me a couple of lines, and then I did my big speech. Before the third time, when the camera was going to roll, Lamont gave me two tips.

"Miss Barton-Poole, think of the camera not as something mechanical, but as the eyes of the audience. And the audience is looking right into your eyes, up close. You needn't speak so that the back row of a theater can hear you. Just talk to Edwin. He's right there next to camera. Don't make any facial expression unless you would use it when speaking to a good friend only two feet away."

I wondered if the guy was trying to sabotage me. How would the audience see me acting if I didn't do anything with my face?

So we did the scene one more time, and now the camera was rolling. I got through without any mistakes and figured it went pretty good. When we got to the end of the scene, Lamont called "Cut!" and the cameraman turned off the camera. No one said anything, and the cameraman wouldn't look me in the eye.

Lamont spoke up, addressing Edwin and the camera guy. "Gentlemen, would you excuse us while I speak with Miss Barton-Poole?" The cameraman turned off the set lights as he walked away from the scene.

Lamont motioned that I should sit, but I was too excited.

"Well, that went pretty good, don't you think?" I said. "I didn't forget any of the lines, turned my head right toward the light the way the cameraman said I should on that last sentence."

"You've paid me a substantial sum of money for my honest opinion of your chance of success as an actress in motion pictures," said Lamont. "I've run such screen tests for hundreds of actors and actresses over the last several years, so I bring a certain level of experience to this."

"What I need to know is, could I be the next Harlow? I've got the looks and the body, and my hair turned out great as a platinum blonde."

He shook his head. "Here it is. I think you could have a career in Hollywood if you are content with background work and the occasional small speaking role, much as you have been doing for the past three years. And that will last as long as your beauty lasts. I don't see any ability on your part to project to the audience. And when you try to project, it is even worse. It is overdone."

"Are you saying I don't have any talent?" I was getting steamed.

"No, I didn't say that. Only that the talent you have has taken you as far as you're going to get."

"Oh."

I had been right not to bring Al along. I didn't want him to see my dream crushed like this.

I hate it when people feel sorry for me.

two~
The Ambassador Hotel
Labor Day 1932

SO NOW WE knew what our play was going to be. The next step was figuring how to get the photos to Mayer and arranging for payment without getting caught.

We found a guy who would dress in a delivery uniform and take the goods to Mayer's home over the long Labor Day weekend. We figured that would give him time to stew about the damage the studio would suffer if they lost Harlow.

As to the payment, Al thought he could set up a wire transfer to a buddy from his old gang in New York, a guy who had a banker in his pocket, but I wondered if we could trust the buddy or the banker. Al hadn't seen either of them in a year, and I'd never met the men at all.

"It's not so much that there is honor among thieves," said Al. "It's that each knows I'll kill him if he queers the deal." He laughed, but not in his usual whole-hearted way.

One of Al's good traits is that he knows so much about

how things work, both in finance and crime.

Another one is that he has the stamina of a twenty year old, though he's thirty-two. I often wonder how long that will last if he keeps drinking the way he does. That man can lap it up.

On that night I got called to meet an old client at the Ambassador and picked up a surprise package of a grand. And I didn't have to do a thing for it. I was prepared to give the guy a show if needed, though I wouldn't take a beating again. I didn't tell Al that, since he gets so jealous about such stuff. He has a hard enough time taking the photos without punching the marks.

I think the best thing about a conscience is that other people have them.

~~~

MONDAY ABOUT NOON I got a call from Marshal Lawe. I still call him that, not Petey. Force of habit from Peony Springs, I guess. His voice sounded dead strange.

"Jackie Sue, I need Al to drive you over to an address on Benedict Canyon. I need both of you together, and I need you right away."

Since Petey was a fixer at MGM, this gave me the willies.

"What's up, Petey? Why the rush?"

"I can't talk about it on the telephone. But I need to see you, and it has to happen now."

"It's a holiday. Can't it wait? Al was going to take me down to Santa Monica beach so I can show off my new bathing suit."

His voice got all steely, like when he was talking to the judge, back in Peony Springs.

"Put Al on the telephone." He must have realized he was coming across awful strong, so he added, "Please."

I made a face at Al that let him know something funny was going on and handed him the receiver. Meantime I got myself dressed. Al only talked with Petey a minute, wrote down an address, and hung up.

I turned to him, seeing what he thought we should do.

"I think we've been made," said Al, "but I can't for the life of me see how."

"Should we go meet him?"

He nodded yes and said, "I'm hoping maybe we can cut him in on it, keep the play from going bust." He quick-stepped over to the dresser and got out his Baretta. "But let's hedge our bets a bit. Pack enough clothes for the both of us, in case it's a quick trip we need to be making. Bring your birth certificate, the one saying you're Gayle. I'll bring my jacket with the false lining and have our cash along, as well."

We were motoring in the car inside ten minutes, and I confess I wasn't feeling any too happy. It was the first time I'd been with Al that I'd ever seen him show any nerves at all. It's his self-confidence, not lack of confidence, that usually gets him in trouble.

"Why'd you bring the heater?" I said.

"Call it insurance. If I can't talk my way out of this, it gives us a second exit."

"Blackmail is one thing, it's just a little sport, but I don't care to have blood on my hands. I don't want to be part of any murder."

"It's not a murtherer I am." He gave me a lopsided grin and patted the gun in his pocket. "Just a little extra persuasion."

"If he's on to us, let's just cut and run. I don't want either of us going to jail over some silly photographs."

I didn't want to tell him what was really on my mind, not yet.

"I'm not going to gaol, lass. I have the luck of the Irish."

"Well, I'm not Irish, I'm American." I was being snappish, but I couldn't stop myself. "How much do you think he knows?"

"There's no point in speculating. Let's go meet the man. Things will sort themselves out."

~~~

IT WAS A ritzy area, pretending to be rural with its narrow road lined by oak trees. The houses were big and were surrounded by gardens that looked like they'd had a manicure and trim that morning. I'd seen a map that showed plenty of movie stars lived up Benedict Canyon. I'd hoped to live there myself one day. We slowed down as we neared Eaton Drive.

Petey came out from behind his car and waved us down. He walked over, all business, opened the passenger door and got in the front seat with us. He looked unsettled in a way I hadn't seen before.

Once he was seated inside with us, he seemed at sixes and sevens.

After a moment, Al spoke. "Well, Petey, what's all this rushing around in aid of?"

"I don't know how to say this, exactly. And I'm not sure about your involvement."

Uh-oh, I thought to myself. I felt Al reach his hand into his pocket, getting hold of his pistol.

"Involvement in what?" said Al.

"Just up this next street there's been a murder."

I squeaked with surprise and embarrassed myself

no end. I thought I was ready for anything.

Al looked across me at Marshal, and I could see the wheels turning. "Who's been murdered?"

"Paul Bern. You know—well, maybe you don't—Jean Harlow's husband."

Oh, we knew all right, but neither of us was going to say a word right now.

"The butler found him this morning," Marshal went on, "naked as a jaybird on the floor of his bathroom, lying in a puddle of blood, his brains blown out."

"So who killed him?" I said.

"I don't know, and neither do they. But if I was still a lawman, I'd be questioning Harlow pretty close about now."

"You mean the police aren't questioning her?"

Marshal paused a long time and when he spoke, his voice was strained. "The police haven't been called yet." You could see this last detail really was eating at him. "For one thing."

"What?" I said. "When did this happen?"

"Far as I can estimate, it happened last night, though a coroner might say something else." He paused again, clearly unhappy. "If they ever call him out here."

"You said 'for one thing.' What has this to do with us?" said Al.

And now Marshal really looked like he'd bitten into a sour apple. "The other thing is that Harlow can't be found."

"So that's what really has them worried, isn't it?" said Al.

Marshal nodded and said, "Someone at the studio remembered how much 'Gayle' looks like Harlow. It's my job to get you to pretend to be her until the studio locates her. They'll pay you five thousand for up to three days work, but you'll have to sign some papers swearing you to secrecy."

"That's crazy," I said. "I can't pretend to be someone I don't even know."

"Here's how they want to work it. You just cry and sob and throw yourself on the couch, and it's so bad you can't speak to anyone. They'll get a doctor to come and examine you, and he'll say you're having a nervous breakdown or some such and the police can't question you until you're over the shock."

"Why'd you ask me to drive her over?" said Al.

"Seeing as you two are a couple, I thought it was up to the both of you if you want to get involved." He cleared his throat. "I don't want you to think I'm recommending this."

"I can do it," I said. "Easy money as an actress, and maybe it'll convince them I deserve some bigger parts." Mentally I kicked myself as soon as I said this in front of Al. Why couldn't I let that go?

"Jackie Sue, what you're missing is that it makes you part of a conspiracy to obstruct justice," said Marshal. "If it ever comes out, you'd be in serious trouble."

"Petey, can Jackie Sue and I have a minute to talk this over?" said Al. "Alone."

"Of course. I'll wait in my car. If you want to do this I'll drive you up to Harlow's mother's place and see that you get some of her clothes to wear. A guy named Orsatti, Mayer's errand boy, will meet you there with the money and the papers. Al should be there to witness it and take the cash."

Marshal got out and walked away.

Al and I looked at each other.

"Do you think that Bern saw the pictures and killed himself?" I said, my voice shaking. I wasn't sure I liked the thought of being the cause of that.

"I think he'd be wanting to kill her, not himself," said Al. "I don't believe this is related to us at all." He thought for a moment. "Although it must have lit a bonfire under Mayer to have this happen in the same weekend."

"Should I do it?" I said.

"And isn't it like hiding in plain sight?" He laughed. "I'll put the next part of our plan into action."

Al smiled, looking crafty and happy at the same time. I think he liked the risk as much as the reward.

"We'll have our money by Friday, if I don't miss my guess."

PETEY REPLIES

"The truth is more important
than the facts."
    —*Frank Lloyd Wright*

one~
Eaton Drive
Labor Day 1932

I HATED THE fact that Eddie Mannix, the studio's
number one fixer, could call me any time of the day or
night. When I was a marshal, a call that woke me from a
sound sleep was a call to serve justice. The calls I got now
were about making justice look the other way.

Gladys hadn't said anything to me, but I could tell she
saw it the same way. I always washed it out of my mind
by telling myself it paid the rent and no one was being
hurt. Or not being hurt much.

This particular call came just past eight in the morning.
I was told to meet Whitey Hendry at an address on Eaton
Drive. There was a body involved, and Whitey wanted
my cop's eye to check it out with him.

I got out of a warm bed and began pulling on

my clothes. Gladys stirred and wiggled over close where I sat on the edge of the bed, trying to keep me company.

"What is it this time, Petey? Some drunk actor crashed his car? Studio executives at a drug party with some underage girls?"

"It's worse this time. Paul Bern's dead."

"Paul Bern?"

"You know, he married Jean Harlow a couple of months ago."

Gladys looked worried. "If it was a natural death, they wouldn't need you. Must mean a suicide or a murder."

"That's what I'm afraid of, too."

She looked at me longingly as I finished dressing.

"Petey, you know I'm on your side."

"I know that, dear."

"I trust you to do the right thing."

I was going to remember her saying that again and again during the rest of the day.

~~~

LOUIS MAYER'S LIMOUSINE was pulling out of the steep gravel driveway just as I arrived. I saw Irving Thalberg, the studio's head of production and Mayer's right hand, sitting on a concrete bench talking with a Negro. From the clothes he wore, I took him to be the gardener.

Hendry's car was near the servants' quarters, so I went and parked next to it. The butler, who introduced himself as John Carmichael, told me Hendry was waiting for me in the bedroom and showed me the way.

I saw the body from the hallway. I'd never met Bern myself, but he'd been pointed out to me on the studio lot.

Hendry stepped from around a corner of the bathroom, walking carefully to avoid the blood. I saw the gun lying across the room.

"It's a bad business, Lawe."

"Death always is."

"Take a look and tell me how you see this happening."

I walked carefully around the room, scanning as I went. The bed was rumpled, like someone had sat there, but not turned down as if someone had slept in it.

The gun, a .38, was lying in the middle of the room, ten feet from the body. It looked like someone had dropped it there. I couldn't make out any distinct footprints in the nap of the carpet because too many feet had been walking around, but I saw a difference in the sheen of the fiber near the gun. I brushed my hand across it and felt dampness.

"Somebody try to clean up something here? The carpet's still damp."

Hendry was surprised. "Damp? No, nobody tried to clean anything yet. If it's damp, it's from something else. I'll go ask the butler if he spilled a drink or something when he first discovered the body."

With Hendry out of the room, I knelt down and sniffed the end of the gun barrel. I could smell the burnt gun powder, so I figured this was the weapon that caused Bern's death. I couldn't see any obvious blood droplets on the gun.

I walked into the bathroom. Bern's naked body lay half in a walk-in closet, half on the tile floor. I went on my knees to see if there were powder burns on Bern's right temple, like I'd seen when people were shot at close range. I could see some, but the pattern was a little broad, as if the gun had been some distance away, not tight against the temple. I checked his right hand, checking for blood that might have splattered back if he held the gun to his own head. Nothing.

I stood up next to the body and looked around me. I saw a wet bathing suit in the corner of the room. Maybe that explained the dampness on the carpet. Maybe. I decided I'd sniff the damp spot and see if it had that chlorine smell that swimming pools do.

On one wall, I saw blood spatter and probably some brains, too, with a bullet hole in the middle. We'd probably be able to figure out the path of the bullet from that.

It was beginning to fit together.

Hendry came back in. "Butler said he spilled some coffee he'd been bringing to Bern, but that was near the doorway to the hall. He didn't wipe up anything in the room." He gave me an appraising glance. "So you think you've worked this out?"

"I know how I'd bet with the evidence so far."

"Tell me."

"Bern's in the bathroom taking off his swimming trunks. Someone comes in, uses the pistol we see out there to shoot him in the head. He didn't see it coming, or at least not soon enough to raise his hand to defend himself. Then the shooter drops the gun on his way out of the bedroom. We need to check that gun for fingerprints."

"Know whose gun that is?" said Hendry. "Bern's. He kept it out in the open on the nightstand next to the bed."

"Okay, so the shooter killed him with his own gun. If it was out in the open, he didn't even have to look for it."

"Why do you keep saying he? Something indicate a man did this?"

"Nope. Just force of habit. So where is the wife? What does she say about this?"

"The butler and the cook say they drove Harlow over to her mother's place last night and stayed there to cook dinner for the two women. After they washed up, they came back here and went to bed about ten last night. Harlow spent the rest of the night over there."

"So the Carmichaels didn't hear this? Slept through a gunshot?"

"They say they didn't hear any shot."

"You're holding something back. What did they hear?" I said.

"They heard Bern arguing with a woman and yelling 'Get out of my life.' Then a scream, and a few minutes later a woman runs by, jumps into a limo, and is driven away."

"What woman? Who saw her?"

"Mrs. Carmichael, the cook. Says she doesn't know who it was."

I was not feeling good about this whole setup, so I asked what I knew was the key question.

"Why haven't you called the police? This is a murder scene."

Hendry looked at me for a long time. "MGM is the biggest employer in this city, and the studio makes more profit than General Motors or Ford. Mr. Mayer is the highest paid man in the country, makes more than the President of the United States. What do you think will happen if it turns out that our rising star, just married two months, has killed her husband—who also turns out to be a studio hot shot?"

"It's still a murder."

"I heard he was impotent and he tried to rape her with a dildo on their wedding night."

"That's sad, real sad, but it doesn't change what I see here. What any detective will see."

"Now we're at the heart of it, Lawe. Mayer and Thalberg have decided that we can get the public behind Harlow, if it turns out her husband was impotent and killed himself over the shame of it all. It'll be tragic, all right, but it won't kill the box office."

"Are you serious?"

"And I want your cop's eye to help me set the scene, so the police come to the conclusion we want them to."

I heard Thalberg come in the front door. He stood out in the hall. I guess he was squeamish about seeing dead bodies, just not squeamish about covering up murder.

"How much longer do you men need before I call the police?" said Thalberg.

"At least a couple of hours," said Hendry. "Have you talked to the gardener, the cook, the butler?"

"They're squared away. Also a couple friends of Bern came by. They'd already heard about his death. Sam Marx and the neighbor, Slavko Vorkapich. I sent them home, said there'd been a tragedy. Sam will have to sit in at the meeting in the morning with Mayer and the other producers."

"Where's Harlow?" I said. I had a bad feeling about this. "We need to talk with her." I hoped that if we got her here at the site with the police around, she might just tell the whole story. I've seen plenty of confessions that were prompted by the suspect being at the scene.

Thalberg's face froze up. "I can't find her. I called her mother and she said Jean's not there. I told her Bern was dead and she became hysterical. I tried to get her husband, Bello, on the telephone, but the housekeeper told me he's out of town with Gable, dove hunting."

"Couple of those five-foot-three, hundred and ten pound doves, no doubt," said Hendry.

Hendry and Thalberg exchanged a look. They knew something else, but they weren't about to discuss it in front of me.

"I found a book out by the entry. Looks like something guests sign when they come to dinner," said Thalberg. "There's a note I think we can use to support the suicide story."

~~~

WHAT I DID next makes me ashamed. Hendry and I shifted the position of the body so the pool of blood was still by the head, but more like he was facing the mirror. They thought it would seem like he was imitating a suicide scene from a recent movie.

Hendry found a bottle of Harlow's perfume and sprinkled it over Bern's body pretty liberal. Said it would make his death more poignant, because he was thinking of her.

Hendry got some gun oil from his car and wiped the pistol down with it, smearing whatever fingerprints were there. He placed the weapon next to Bern's right hand.

I started to feel sick to my stomach and went to the kitchen for a glass of water. I found a broken crystal goblet with some blood smeared on it.

When I told Hendry about it he said the gardener had found it outside. He was distracted as he read and re-read the guest book entries, and told me to me talk with the gardener about where exactly it was found, in case there were other items to be "squared away."

I walked down the short hill to the servants' quarters and found the gardener, Clifton Davis. I asked him about the goblet.

"Yes, I found two of them this morning as I getting ready to clean around the swimming pool. An empty champagne bottle, too."

"Was one of the goblets already broken?"

"Yes, sir. I took it inside to see if they might mend it later. There was blood on the goblet and also some by the side of the pool. I already cleaned that up. It was right next to where I found the woman's yellow bathing suit."

"Was that a suit belonging to Mrs. Bern?" I said.

"I can't say for sure, but I'd never seen her wear it before."

"You know, the police are going to want to talk with you."

He looked uneasy at this. It's my experience that most colored men don't like talking with the police.

"Mr. Thalberg already told me what I should say, sir" said Davis.

"Is that so?"

He nodded and I left him to his work. When I got back inside Hendry was bent over the dining room table. He had a ruler and a pen knife and was cutting part of a page from the guest book. He concentrated hard enough that he had the tip of his tongue sticking out. If I wasn't so upset with what was going on, I would have thought it funny.

He had just cut the cropped page free when the telephone rang. He went into the next room to answer it, and I took the chance to read the page. It was an odd sort of note.

Dearest Dear,
Unfortunately this is the
only way to make good the
frightful wrong I have done you
and to wipe out my abject
humiliation. I love you,
  Paul.
You understand that last night
was only a comedy

The last sentence broke off without a period, like there was more to follow. Part of the note was missing, and I looked into the book to see what was on the remainder of the page.

What was written there referred to a dinner party that had gone bad and how Bern realized that Harlow didn't like the house he had built for her.

This isn't a suicide note at all, I thought to myself. *So what am I going to do about this?*

I stood there, paralyzed. Trying to choose between the job I was doing and what I thought was the truth.

I tore out the missing piece as quietly as I could and slipped it into my pocket.

Hendry came back and took the note and the guest book from my hand. In return he gave me a bit of paper with a name, phone number, and address written in pencil.

"I'll finish up in here, Lawe. I have a new task for you. Thalberg called to say there's a gal we can use as a double for Harlow. She goes by the name of Gayle Barton. She's done a number of bit parts and background work at the studio. We want you to get her over to the home of Harlow's mother. The mother's married to a guy by the name of Marino Bello. Tell the Barton girl that Harlow is in seclusion due to grief, but we need her to appear before the press, just on the front porch of the Bello house."

"You're kidding," I said.

Hendry gave me a vexed look. "No."

I didn't let on that I knew 'Gayle.'

"What is she supposed to do, impersonate Harlow, talk to the press?" I said.

"No. She's not to say a cotton-pickin' word to anyone. Not a single word. All she has to do is cry and carry on like she's out of her mind with grief. There's five grand in it for her, and we'll send a contract by messenger over to the Bello place."

I got on the telephone with Jackie Sue and arranged to meet with her and Al.

Something told me they'd prob'ly go along.

Just like me.

Then I tried to tell myself I was just doing my job.

two~
City of Lost Angels
September 8, 1932

IT HAD TAKEN but three days to smear the memory of Paul Bern. The MGM publicity department went into high gear, feeding rumors to the tabloids. Rumors about Bern's violent temper and the beatings he had given Harlow. Rumors about his impotence. Rumors about a first wife that he had driven insane and left in an asylum. Rumors about his financial losses and looming bankruptcy. Rumors about his rape of Harlow on their wedding night.

Was Bern the monster they made him out to be? Hardly likely, or else why did Harlow marry him. And why did so many actresses swear he was their best friend and confessor?

It made me sick. My stomach started hurting all day long, and I feared I was getting an ulcer.

And the LAPD! They had come in, taken a cursory look around, then swallowed what Thalberg and Hendry told them. They didn't even bother to take fingerprints from the crystal goblets. If the coroner did an autopsy, it must have been done quick, and with his eyes closed.

I was told to attend the coroner's inquest on Thursday and make sure nothing funny was said by the witnesses. The inquest was held at the mortuary that was preparing his body for the funeral.

I sat through it. Didn't take more than three hours to tell the tale.

They called the butler, the cook, the gardener, the chauffeur, Irving Thalberg, and even more to the stand. Every one of them told "facts" that I knew to be false. The time of discovery of the body was changed from before seven a.m. till after noon. Thalberg supposedly called the police at noon, but the lines were busy, and he couldn't get through for forty-five minutes. There was no late night visitor mentioned, no argument heard, no broken goblet found, no woman hurrying into the darkness.

On the other hand, Frank Nance, our county coroner, asked Harlow's stepdad if he had seen Bern the night of the death. He hadn't. Did he know when Bern died? No, it could have been Sunday or Monday. Did he know the cause of death?

I twitched in my seat. If Bello hadn't been there and hadn't seen him, how could he know the cause of death? However, it seems that he did. He said it was suicide. And this was the first "witness" on the stand.

Every subsequent witness was asked about Bern's mental state and whether he had discussed suicide. The coroner's jury was being led down the garden path.

When the coroner questioned Thalberg, MGM's second in command, it went like this—

CORONER: Was Bern working under severe strain at times?

THALBERG: Yes, he was.

As a movie producer? Yeah, probably, I thought.

CORONER: Did you notice that he had been nervous at times?

THALBERG: Yes, he had been nervous at times and he would get better.

CORONER: Did he ever discuss the suicide problem with you as a scientific fact or in any way?

THALBERG: Yes, he did.

They went on like that for some time. Thalberg said that he and Bern had discussed suicide many times. Since the both of them produced movies and had scripts that concerned suicide, that seemed an easy statement to make. Thalberg also mentioned that some of Bern's family members had killed themselves.

I had the feeling someone had written a script for the coroner, with both the questions and answers predetermined.

But the biggest surprise of the inquest was when Jean Harlow and Bern's brother Henry didn't appear at all, even though their presence had been requested. Henry sent word that he was exhausted from his cross-country train trip. Made it sound like he was being excused from school, not an inquest into the death of his brother.

Harlow's doctor sent a note to Frank Nance, the county coroner:

> My dear Mr. Nance,
> Miss Jean Harlow has been under my care since Monday, September 5th, 1932, and has been suffering a severe nervous collapse. Her appearance before the coroner's jury would severely endanger her life.
> Sincerely,
> Robert Helm Kennicut

To no one's surprise the coroner's jury ruled the death to be a suicide, with motive undetermined. MGM assigned a guard to the coffin; why, I don't know.

~~~

I MET WITH Henry Bern after the inquest. He had come back from New York where he had been tracking down Paul's ex-wife, Dorothy Millette. Well, sorta ex-wife. They had lived together ten years but never actually been married. And then she spent several years in the looney bin.

It seems she had been cured recently and wanted to resume her marriage to Paul. Except now he was legally married to Jean Harlow. Dorothy had decided to come to Los Angeles and meet with Paul. Henry had been trying to talk her out of it.

"So where is she now?" I said to Henry.

"She's staying at a hotel in San Francisco. Paul sends her a monthly stipend, so she's okay for money."

"You think she's going to contest the will or anything like that?"

"She assured me nothing like that would ever happen," said Henry.

It was my job to see if any of this was going to blow up in the press, but it looked to be pretty well under wraps.

I went to Bern's funeral. It seemed like half of Hollywood was there, and it was an MGM production from start to finish. I heard there was twenty-five thousand dollars spent on just the flowers. There were the usual eulogies, which sounded kinda off kilter, since they all thought he killed himself.

And then there was a finale like I never heard of before

and hope never to see again. At the end of the service the funeral director said we could all take a final look at Paul Bern and say our last goodbye.

Some mechanism began to hum, and the casket rotated until it stood upright. When it did, half the lid slid back and revealed Bern, made up the way they do with bodies, especially in Hollywood. His hair cut and combed, the makeup laid on thick and bright. It was sort of like he was standing inside a confessional booth looking out at the audience.

Harlow screamed and began to sob. The actor Jack Gilbert puked all over Clark Gable's shoes, and the both of them rushed out the exit.

I don't think I really knew what excess was till I got to Hollywood.

~~~

THE BODY WAS cremated right after the ceremony. I guess they thought that would put an end to the story.

I met with my boss, Hendry, the next day. I was feeling pretty low. We talked in his office on the MGM lot.

"So I guess that's taken care of," I said. "As long as the DA keeps his nose out of it."

He gave me a kind of wintry smile. "Mr. Fitts knows which side his bread is buttered on. So does the coroner."

"Does it bother you to be involved in such things?"

He lit up an Old Gold, took his time doing it. Picked a strand of tobacco from his tongue. "How many years we been in this Depression? Three? Does it look like it's getting any better to you?"

"I don't follow you."

"The movies are the only real escape most folks have. They get to forget their troubles for two hours. Watch beautiful people do beautiful things. We can't let the petty behavior of our actors take that away from the American public."

Petty behavior? Murder?

I left his office and went to get a Danish. I wasn't sure if Hendry really believed that bilge or was saying it to soothe my conscience.

As I drank my joe, I wondered how I had come to such a pass. I didn't feel I needed money this much. But on the other hand, Gladys deserved it. She'd had a tough life, and I didn't want it to get tougher because her husband was unemployed.

I went home to talk with my wife.

GLADYS AT HOME

"Life is just one damned thing after another."
—*Frank Ward O'Malley*

one~
Our Bungalow
September 1932

JACKIE SUE SURPRISED me by showing up without calling ahead that day. Personally, I didn't feel like we had all that much in common, but I guess the fact that we had lived in Peony Springs at the same time, and that Al knew Petey, counted for something with her.

I made coffee and got out some of the zucchini bread I'd baked the night before. She ate the first piece so quick I decided I'd just leave the loaf on the table for us both to nibble on.

"I figure Marshal—sorry, I mean Petey—must have told you about the part I played in this Bern and Harlow mess," she said.

He'd told me, and I knew it didn't sit right with him. I decided I didn't need to respond to this.

"I got five thousand to do nothing but cry and stay bundled up in a scarf, sunglasses, and a robe for three days. I won't have to work for a while."

Five thousand dollars? That would solve a lot of our problems. Petey's only making sixty-five a week.

"I'm happy for you, I guess," I said. "Did you feel funny pretending to be her?"

"I'm an actress. It's just a part, and now it's over."

She cut her third piece of my zucchini bread, slathered it with butter, and began to attack it with her fork. Something was on her mind.

"How's Al doing?" I said. "Petey hasn't heard from him in a few days."

She looked a little unsettled at this. "He flew to New York on business yesterday. He should get there tomorrow."

"He flew instead of taking the train? That must have cost a pretty penny," I said.

"He's come into an inheritance and had to go to Manhattan to collect it." She took another bite of the bread. "It's a lot of money, so the plane ticket wasn't a problem."

"Does that mean congratulations are in order?" I thought having money meant they'd be getting married, but something else made her blush deeply.

"Does it already show that much?"

"Does what show?" And then I got it. "You're going to have a baby? Bless you, child." She chewed her lip a bit and when she didn't reply, I went on. "Is this a surprise? Something you didn't plan for?"

"No, I knew what I was doing. At least I thought I did. But now— Well, that's why I wanted to talk to you. I'm not certain if I should have it. Maybe I should, you know, get rid of it."

"What are you talking about?"

"I'm not sure Al has what it takes to be a good father,

what with all his scheming." She got choked up and couldn't go on.

I could see her point, remembering everything Petey had told me about his adventures with Al. But I knew better than to voice that opinion to a pregnant woman. And then she piped up again.

"No, that's not it at all," said Jackie Sue. "It's not him, it's me! I'm not sure if I'll make a good mother." And she burst into tears.

I put my arm around her and let her boohoo and talk nonsense for a while. She finally cried herself out, and I felt I could ask her more.

"What is it that scares you the most about this?"

"I think he might just take all that money and run off to Brazil without me."

All that money? I realized something big was in the works and was just as sure that she wasn't going to give me all the details. "Brazil?"

"We'd been talking about going there to live."

"Why would you want to move to Brazil?" I said.

"It's not me, so much. It's Al. He thinks he'd be safer there." She looked me straight in the eye. "Al has kind of a checkered past. He's been involved with—well, with criminal elements."

"And going to Brazil would make him safe?"

"We wouldn't tell anyone where we were. And besides, there's no extradition treaty between Brazil and the United States."

She knew that word at her age? She must have had some serious discussions with Al. And extradition had nothing to do with the mob, it meant some kind of federal crime.

"Maybe you shouldn't be telling me this," I said. "Not if it's really gonna be a secret, you know."

"But I want my baby to be an American citizen." And she burst into tears again. I saw the coffee pot was empty and thought this would be a good time to switch to chamomile tea. I got up and set the pot brewing while she quieted down.

"Al is Irish. He never became a citizen. I'm not old enough to get my passport without my parents' permission, and *that's* not going to happen. My only other ID is a fake British birth certificate. So if my child were born in Brazil, he'd be Irish, Brazilian, or British—but not American. I don't want my child to be a foreigner! No one likes foreigners!"

"Have you talked this over with Al?" I was betting she hadn't, or she wouldn't be talking about an abortion. But on the other hand I knew she was also smart enough to fake "losing" it without Al getting wise to it.

"Early this morning, between hops."

"Hops?"

"Those cross-country flights, you know? The plane has to stop every four hours to refuel. He called me on the telephone from some airfield in Dallas. The connection was pretty good, considering he was a thousand miles away."

"So he knows you're pregnant. Was he happy to hear the news?"

"He seemed happy, but how can you really know if a man's telling the truth unless you can talk to him naked, face to face."

The image I had of Petey conducting a police interrogation that way made me smile. Jackie Sue saw it and went from tearful to angry in about one second flat.

"This isn't funny, Gladys. I'm facing a difficult decision here. I thought I could come to you for help. Don't you go laughing at me."

"I'm sorry. I just thought about Petey questioning a suspect with them both naked, and—"

I didn't get any further because Jackie Sue started laughing so hard she had to hurry off to the bathroom.

I poured the tea for us and put the last slice of bread on her dish. I hoped she wouldn't eat it, because I was getting peckish myself. Jackie Sue came back with her face washed and her hair brushed. She sat down and tackled her fourth piece of zucchini bread.

"You better take your time, girl. There ain't no more after that."

She put her fork down and swallowed. "Al said he'd go on ahead, put our money into a good bank, find us a place to live, hire servants, and have everything ready."

"Ready?"

"He thinks I should have the baby down there. But I told him I wanted to have the baby in America and then join him when I could travel."

I saw this is where it could get ticklish. "And he said?"

"He told me he'd send me an allowance of three hundred dollars a month to live on until his son and I could join him."

"His son, eh? Sounds just like a man, like it's not fifty-fifty it's gonna be a baby girl."

She drained her teacup, wiped her mouth with a napkin, and pushed her chair back. Either I had given her all the advice she needed, or she was going to find a restaurant that served an early lunch.

"Thanks so much, Gladys. It really helped talking to you. I'll ring and let you know when I've decided what to do."

I cried for a while after she left. And then I telephoned Aunt Naomi. She cried, too.

~~~

PETEY TOLD ME all about Bern's funeral and my jaw dropped so far I was in danger of swallowing flies. But he looked like something was eating him from the inside out.

"I don't think I can do this anymore, Gladys."

I sat very still, afraid of what was coming.

"I know I said I was through with the law, but this is, is—well, it's just too much."

"It wasn't you killed anybody, Petey."

"But I covered up the fact that a murder was committed."

"Put those on the scales of justice, and I know which one is the heaviest."

"Every day I'm there I undermine the things I used to believe in."

"You still believe in them. You have the best heart of any man I know."

"It's not like it was back in Massachusetts, when I was looking the other way so some moonshiner could sell his goods. That didn't hurt anybody." He was angry with himself. "But maybe that was just me being ignorant, starting down the broad highway to Hell."

"Are you thinking of going to the police?"

"I was until I found out the DA is probably on the MGM payroll. Most likely the coroner, too."

"You're just a country mouse in the city."

"So I've been told." He nodded, looking into space.

"Can't you let it be?" In my heart I knew he couldn't, but how could we—

"A mouse can get into a lot of places you don't expect it to, see things you didn't know it saw." He turned to look at me. "I heard Bern had an ex-wife. And now she's gone missing from a ferry boat near San Francisco."

"What can *you* do about it if the police are in on the fix?" I said.

"I've started my own evidence book on this."

"How will that make a difference?"

"Fact is, I already put that leftover fragment of the suicide note on the desk of the *LA Times* crime reporter. Did it anonymous." He put his face in his hands and massaged his temples. "I'm hoping that he'll put some steam behind reopening the coroner's inquest on Bern's death."

"If you have to quit your job, you know I'll understand," I said.

"We can't live on what you make waitressing. And besides, I'm supposed to be taking care of you, not the other way around."

I smiled at that. It was Petey to the core.

"I'll look again to see if I can't find a job cooking, make better money," I said.

"I want you to cook because you're a great cook. Besides, waiting tables is too hard on your feet."

"But I'm not going to quit my waitress job until I have something better. Maybe that's the way you can do it, too. Start looking, asking around."

"I thought about being a private investigator," said Petey.

"And spend your time pulling people's dirty laundry

out for everyone to see? That doesn't sound like you."

And we talked on into the evening, working the problem around, chewing it over good. In the end we decided to put his change of jobs on hold. These were hard times and he made good money.

About nine that night the phone rang. Petey groaned, afraid it was another MGM task that would take him away all night long. He answered and looked kind of funny. He held out the receiver and put his hand over the mouthpiece.

"It's for you. Jackie Sue's calling."

I took the receiver and let Jackie Sue tell me all about the new passport Al was arranging for her—an American passport that showed how she was old enough to travel on her own.

"We're going to Rio de Janeiro, Gladys. I mean to say, isn't that just too exciting?"

"It surely is, Jackie Sue."

"And my boy will be an American citizen, since I'm one."

"You sure that's the way it works? Doesn't Al have an Irish passport?"

"He'll do the right thing or I'll know the reason why," said Jackie Sue.

I could hear the hesitation in her voice and she rang off shortly.

I told Petey all about Jackie Sue's visit and speculated with him about what devilment Al was up to. Petey said Al was a wonder, and so was Jackie Sue.

"You think I ought to let her parents know where she's living now, put their minds at ease?"

"I expect she'll be getting in touch with them herself pretty soon."

"How's that?"

"She's going to have Al's baby."

He just sat there with his mouth agape, until I had to giggle.

"But she's only sixteen!" he said at last. "Well, maybe seventeen. Do you remember what her birthday is?"

"These things happen. And no, I don't know when her birthday is. Anyway, she'll be making up a new birth date for herself when the nurse fills out the birth certificate."

"I thought that girl had her heart set on being a movie star."

"When a woman's going to have a child she begins to see things different. Her body does some of the thinking."

Petey pondered that for a bit and then muttered, half to himself,

"A baby! In these times. And those two as parents! She and Al are probably thinking up new con games using the baby."

I waited until he settled down. I leaned against him and felt the solid strength of his shoulder.

He's a good man, a strong man, and I know he loves me as much as I love him. He makes me feel safe. And I'm glad.

I looked into his face until he knew something was up.

"What?" he said, very soft.

"We're going to have a baby, too."

THE END

HISTORY AND ACCURACY

I have done my best to maintain historical accuracy concerning all the characters who really lived: Irving Thalberg, Paul Bern, Jean Harlow, Coroner Frank Nance, DA Buron Fitts, Harlow's stepfather Marino Bello, and the domestic staff of Paul Bern—the Carmichaels and Clifton Davis. However, there were a great many rumors about these people at the time, and it is not always possible to distinguish fact from fantasy.

For those interested in the case, there is a wealth of information. Two books that I found very useful, but which come to opposite conclusions about Bern's suicide are:

Deadly Illusions: Jean Harlow and the Murder of Paul Bern by Samuel Marx and Joyce Vanderveen (Dell, 1990)

Bombshell: The Life and Death of Jean Harlow by David Stenn (Lightning Bug Press, 2000)

Marx, a close friend of Paul Bern and an insider at MGM, was at the Bern home early on Labor Day morning. He was able to contact his old friends from MGM and build an convincing picture of the events before and after Bern's death.

Stenn has written a number of biographies of Hollywood celebrities and does an excellent job of finding surviving friends and relatives of Bern and Harlow.

I also made extensive use of contemporary accounts in newspapers and tabloids, as well as transcripts of court proceedings. The depiction of "charity" girls, Prohibition, drug usage, the jazz scene, gambling ships, and the sexual revolution of the twenties are drawn from contemporary accounts. Although I have my characters visiting the *Johanna Smith* in August of 1932, the ship had burned shortly before this. However, this particular ship worked better for my story than others that were then moored off Los Angeles.

As to the LAPD, District Attorney, and County Coroner in 1932 Los Angeles, the corruption in Los Angeles politics during the twenties and early thirties was second only to Chicago.

The mystery of Paul Bern's death was never adequately resolved, despite two more coroner's inquests. It was never in the interests of MGM that it should be. It *was* true that he had a common law wife, Dorothy Millette, who had been incarcerated in a mental asylum for several years. She did make a recovery and wanted to be back in his life. She was jealous of Harlow, feeling that Jean was having the career that belonged to Dorothy. She committed "suicide" by leaping unobserved from a ferry boat, the day after Bern's death was announced in the papers.

However, there is also strong evidence that she visited Bern the night of his death. There are conflicting reports of a three way violent confrontation between Bern, Harlow, and Millette that night.

There is no confirming evidence of Harlow's whereabouts after the Carmichaels returned to the Bern home. There is only Harlow's mother's word for her daughter's activities. Harlow did not go to her home on Eaton Drive the morning that Paul's death was reported, only a short drive from her mother's house. Instead she went into seclusion, so guarded that the police were unable to speak to her until after the funeral.

And *some* unidentified woman, heavily veiled, did take a limousine from the Bern home to San Francisco, leaving the scene at two in the morning.

There is just time enough for Harlow to get to Dorothy's hotel, confront her, and return late the next day—explaining why she was missing early on Labor Day morning.

Or it is time enough for Dorothy to flee the scene before her "suicide" the next day.

Last Word from That Other Author, Bruce Cook

In 2006 my first novel, *Philippine Fever*, was published. It gave me great satisfaction and joy to see my name on the spine of a book in my local bookstore.

To celebrate, I Googled myself...and discovered that there were three other authors named Bruce Cook. Surprised (and a little horrified at the coincidence), I then researched how common my name really was.

My university had granted degrees to 35 other Bruce Cooks. There are four others in the film industry, where I have worked for almost forty years. There were three Bruce R. Cooks of the exact same age with PhDs.

I attended a mystery convention the following year. As I sat in the author signing room after having been a panelist, a man approached me with an armload of books to sign. I took a look. Nope, I hadn't written any of them. There were other crime novels, books of criticism, westerns, some erotica...a nice eclectic mix. And all written by this or that Bruce Cook.

I realized that one of the Bruce Cooks represented in the pile was already deceased. It was a moment fraught with embarrassment for both the fan and myself. He didn't bother to buy my sole current book.

After the conference I did some more Internet research. Bruce Cooks by the score showed up, of all ages and occupations, on every continent, of every race and religion, both living and dead.

When I got to Bruce Cook the porn star, I realized it was time to come up with a pseudonym for my next novel. This pretty much ended the celebration stage of having my name on the spine.

My second novel, *Blood Harvest*, came out in 2008,

written under the pseudonym Brant Randall. Randall is my middle name and Brant is a favorite hard-boiled character of mine from Ken Bruen's novels. I researched ahead of time to make sure there were no other Brant Randalls writing books.

Of course it meant that I was trying to establish a new brand for myself, and that those readers who had liked *Philippine Fever* would have no way of knowing my new nom de plume. The new name also drew some criticism from my parents, wife, and publisher, all of whom thought my real name was fine.

That's when I had the brainstorm. Bruce and Brant would collaborate on my third novel. That way they could each draw upon their former readers. They could share the writing load. They could split the electricity bill for the computer. They could get a timeshare. They could… Well, you get the picture.

I can't say it has been easy. Bruce and Brant don't always get along.

I just hope it doesn't come down to a lawsuit.

Bruce Cook
one among many

P.S. Let me know what you think about the story. You can write me at:
doccook@earthlink.net
or catch me online at:
www.brucecookonline.com
or www.brantrandallonline.com